The very first match of the season and Tarenton High basketball team should be steaming ahead to the regional and state championships. But not only is the Garrison team stronger than theirs but Tarenton's supporters start cheering the enemy cheerleaders' routine. Then Nancy falls in love – with Ben Adamson, the captain of Garrison! When fights break out on the basketball court, it's the last straw. Nancy is in the centre of the furore and friends and enemies alike make her life a misery.

D0783919

Caroline B. Cooney

CHEERLEADERS

⑤

All the Way

Hippo Books
Scholastic Publications Ltd
London

Scholastic Publications Ltd.,
10 Earlham Street, London WC2H 9LN, UK

Scholastic Inc.,
730 Broadway, New York, NY 10003, USA

Scholastic Tab Publications Ltd.,
123 Newkirk Road, Richmond Hill,
Ontario L4C 3G5, Canada

Ashton Scholastic Pty. Ltd.
PO Box 579, Gosford, New South Wales,
Australia

Ashton Scholastic Ltd.,
165 Marua Road, Panmure, Auckland 6,
New Zealand

First published by Scholastic Inc. USA

First published in UK by Scholastic Publications Ltd.,
1986
Copyright © 1985 by Caroline B. Cooney

ISBN 0 590 70607 1

Printed and bound in Great Britain by
Cox & Wyman Ltd, Reading

CHAPTER

Mary Ellen Kirkwood stepped out in front of the other five cheerleaders; placed her long, slim legs in a V; tossed her head; and cupped her hands around her mouth.

The eyes of five hundred basketball fans were fixed on her, waiting for the cheer. The crowd was screaming already. They were full of energy and excitement, and the cheer would channel their screams into a pounding rhythm.

She knew how beautiful she was with her golden hair gleaming under the hot lights of the Tarenton High gymnasium. No colors could be better for her fair complexion than the white and scarlet of her uniform.

How I love being a cheerleader! Mary Ellen

thought. "All the way!" she yelled at the crowd.

The din in the gymnasium was deafening. Nobody could possibly have heard those three words, not even the other five Varsity cheerleaders facing Mary Ellen. But they could read her lips, and Tarenton fans knew all the cheers and loved them. They would join in.

She did not glance behind her. She knew the coaches were arguing fiercely with the referee, the boys tensely poised to continue the game or come to blows. Whichever side lost this decision was going to fly into a rage.

But Mary Ellen herself was winning.

This hour, this moment, she was Number One. She had it all.

Looks, figure, brains — those she had worked on all her life. But this year she was captain of Varsity. She was the girl with the scarlet carnation pinned to her white wool sweater. Four hundred thirty-seven girls in Tarenton High and she — only she — had such a badge of success.

But there was more.

Behind her, pacing, was Donny Parrish, captain of the basketball team that would take Tarenton to the regional and state championships. Donny Parrish, with more points this season than any single boy in the region — except the cocaptain of the opposite team, Ben Adamson.

Donny: tall, muscular, handsome, and — maybe — hers.

Donny had not dated in the six months since

2

his beloved girl friend moved away. Last week he had invited a girl on his first date after all that time.

And the girl was Mary Ellen Kirkwood.

She smiled with delight just thinking about it.

Beaming at the crowd, thrilled with herself, Mary Ellen started the cheer rhythm with two sharp, geometric gestures. At either end of the squad lineup, the two boys who made Varsity so spectacular stepped farther out, motioned high and wide, and then each girl did a quick sidestep. Mary Ellen stepped into the opening this created. On her third gesture, they swiveled as sharply as a color guard turning a corner, raised their fists in a victory salute, and began the cheer that Tarenton fans wanted to scream:

Roadway, runway, *rail*way!
Make this game our vict'ry day.
Allllll the way! *Allllll* the way!
Not just halfway — *cut out* the horseplay!
Make this game our vict'ry day.
Allllll the way! *Allllll* the way!
Yeaaaaah, Tarenton!

But the finest cheering in America wasn't going to sway this referee. The decision went against Tarenton. Garrison, the enemy, would get two free throws.

A massive scream of protest rose from the throats of five hundred Tarenton fans on the west

3

side of the gym, matched by shouts of triumph from the Garrison crowd.

They had a particularly stupid pair of referees this game. Of all games to draw dunces! Garrison had bitterly fought Tarenton for the regional championships for years now — high school basketball was very important in their part of the country. So you would think that the league organizers would have been sure to send their best to this game. But no. They had sent two men who couldn't distinguish between a basketball and a bowling ball.

Tarenton was on its collective feet, yelling unprintable names and waving fists. The three policemen assigned to the game were shifting from the gymnasium doors to the edge of the bleachers. Everyone knew that the worst thing would be for the cops actually to get involved. That would be the spark that would set the actual fire. So far it was only words and gestures. One more problem and there would be fists.

Now the score was close. There were dangerously few moments left in the game. This decision might well end in an enemy victory.

Enemy.

A word for war.

But this year, it was true.

The animosity between Tarenton and Garrison had reached an appalling level. Although there were decades of traditional rivalry between the two schools, there had never been a time when there was so much open anger at games.

It began during football and soccer. Fistfights, bloody noses, a dislocated jaw, and a lot of anonymous obscenities screamed from the sidelines.

The local paper ran editorials: "What is happening in our schools? Are we teaching our children violence?" The principal, the vice-principal, coaches, teachers — they all lectured the kids. Nobody knew what to do about the situation. With each game the hostility relentlessly accelerated.

Right now you could feel violence in the air, ready to explode into an attack.

Mary Ellen had devised a particular signal for her squad. As the Tarenton fans stood up in their seats, and several older boys gave every sign of being about to stomp down the bleachers and beat the referee to a pulp, she got her squad started in a very complex, wide-ranging cheer. It involved twists and spins, side slides and pikes.

What it was was a moving fence. A human barricade of waving arms, scarlet-wrapped legs, and rustling pompons — six Varsity cheerleaders effectively blockading the court and distracting the eye.

Actually, this wasn't an appropriate time for the cheer. In fact the words to this particular cheer were rather stupid and had nothing to do with anything. But then, Mary Ellen reflected, a lot of cheers were like that. What did roadways,

5

railways, and runways have to do with basketball games? But they kept the fans happy.

Hopefully this cheer would keep the fans off the gym floor as well, and help prevent the spill of blood.

Especially, Mary Ellen thought adoringly, Donny's blood.

Donny was in a peculiar position. Having brought Tarenton to victory in every single game so far this season, he was expected to do so again tonight, against Garrison. If they lost, even by a single point (especially by a single point) Tarenton would be furious with Donny. No matter that he'd racked up nineteen points in this game; no matter that he so carefully helped the others set up their own plays.

What counted was winning.

Winning against Garrison.

Mary Ellen shivered inside her thick, white wool sweater. The pressure was almost unbearable. She felt responsible for the game, as if her throat, her cries, her flashing colors could clinch the score. How must Donny be feeling? *He* had to beat Ben Adamson of Garrison.

The two captains were somewhat alike. Both towered over the rest of the players. Ben was probably a few inches taller and quite a few pounds heavier than Donny. But Ben was beaky like a hawk, with oddly stooped shoulders near the top of his six-and-a-half-feet height. Ben looked like a burned-out criminal. The cheer-leaders had once joked about Ben.

"Not a future athlete of America," Olivia said. "A future *felon* of America."

Donny was rather wholesome looking. Rather. Not completely. Both boys had developed a need to win that surpassed their other characteristics. It came through in everything they did. There was nothing sweet or friendly in their dispositions.

Mary Ellen loved that antagonism, that determination. She had much the same spirit herself, although it didn't show so clearly. All her life she had wanted to be Number One. Mary Ellen — the poor kid in the lousy neighborhood, whose mother was a clerk and whose father drove a bus. Mary Ellen — who did laundry for the neighbors to earn spending money.

Well, tonight, Mary Ellen truly was Number One. There could not be a single girl in the huge audience who was not eaten up with envy over Mary Ellen Kirkwood.

She had known she would love such a position, but she had not known how *much* she would love it. It permeated her every thought, spreading through her life like a gas. Invisible, but everywhere. She breathed it in like oxygen. It was her own private victory over the world.

The game continued.

The fans relaxed slightly, their wrath slowed by the outlet of cheering.

Mary Ellen signaled the squad to take a much-deserved rest. All six sank to the bench in utter exhaustion. Anybody who thought cheerleading was a wimpy sport should have watched Tarenton's Varsity Squad tonight.

No sooner had they hit the wooden seats than Garrison's cheerleading squad leaped to their feet, taking instant advantage of a time-out.

Mary Ellen kicked herself. She should have seen this coming and been ready for it. Now Garrison's cheerleading squad could run out on the floor and do a display, not just a sideline cheer.

Sure enough, the twelve girls from Garrison ran out on the gymnasium center, spread themselves across it, and proceeded to steal the show.

Tarenton had a most unusual squad. First of all, it was coed. There were only a handful of squads in the entire state with boys. Boys added tremendous strength to the squad and allowed for all sorts of lifts and tosses that girls alone could not do. But Tarenton had only six on Varsity, with the rest of the would-be cheerleaders on Pompon Squad.

Garrison had twelve girls. Clad in bright green and vivid yellow, the girls were garish and gaudy. But extremely effective. Unlike Tarenton, which went in for gymnastic-type moves, Garrison was more of a dancing unit. Their moves were intricate but delicate. They were extremely feminine in a totally traditional way. The contrast between the two squads could not have been greater.

Six Garrison girls faced the Garrison side of the gym, and six faced Tarenton. They linked arms, alternating directions, and began one of the most impressive high-kick routines Mary Ellen had ever seen. There was not a single person in the gym ignoring them. Let the basketball players have their huddle! Everybody was taking a break from basketball to appreciate the sight of brilliant symmetry among twelve lovely dancing girls.

Two rows behind her, Mary Ellen heard a Tarenton fan exclaim, "That squad is better than ours!"

If they had accused Mary Ellen of war crimes, she could not have been more upset. *She was Number One!* And therefore, so was the squad she captained.

To her utter horror, several voices agreed. "They're wonderful," came the admiring remarks.

At a time when Garrison was the enemy, people were saying that Garrison's cheerleaders were better. It was all Mary Ellen could do not to turn around and smack their faces. Stinkers, she thought, tears of rage and hurt pricking the back of her eyes. Rotten, no-good judges of cheerleading! What do you know about anything? You traitors. How dare you say Garrison's good at anything at a time like this?

9

Her eyes fixed on Garrison's performance.

They were a very fluid group with sinuous, sensuous motions. Like sirens on the rock, luring sailors to their deaths.

Her squad could never do that. Their two boys were not dancers and — naturally enough — lacked the feminine grace of those girls. Pres Tilford was handsome, dark-blond, muscle-bound male energy. Walt Manners was clown, technique, personality, and height. As for the girls, she, Angie, and Nancy were all dancers, but Olivia was a dazzling gymnast. Lightweight and wiry, Olivia had spectacular tumbling and flipping abilities.

Garrison positively slithered through a routine that seemed to Mary Ellen like pure sex.

"Hey, Kirkwood!" came a shout from way up in the bleachers. "How come *we* can't show off like that?"

Mary Ellen's cheeks burned with humiliation and anger. I don't *want* to show off like that, she thought. And if you were any judge of real ability, you'd put us so far ahead of Garrison it would be laughable.

With a flourish, Garrison wrapped up its display. When Tarenton clapped for them almost as hard as Garrison itself, Mary Ellen's chest tightened with pain. *We're* the best, not Garrison! she thought, agonized.

Vanessa Barlow, who had not made the squad and who was dedicated to getting even, smiled broadly. She threw back her dark, shining hair in a typical Vanessa gesture and called out, "*I* could have added something *you* just don't have — *sex*."

Mary Ellen was not the only cheerleader to feel disgraced. All six moved closer together, deeply upset.

Olivia said, "We're going to learn new routines. I don't care how many hours we have to practice. *Nobody* is ever again going to say we're second best."

One of the very few people in the overheated, smelly gymnasium who was not watching the Garrison cheerleading squad was Nancy Goldstein. A cheerleader for Tarenton, she normally found cheerleading the most absorbing activity, no matter who was cheering. But tonight her dark eyes and her heart were elsewhere. She was gripped by the shoulders and head of Ben Adamson, who towered over everybody but Mary Ellen's Donny.

Nancy thought Ben was the most sexual person she had ever looked at. He claimed more space than other boys out there. Just the way he stood proclaimed ownership. He was like an astronaut putting a flag on the moon. Ben owned the floor, owned that ball, owned the entire game.

Nancy certainly did not want her team to lose. She loved victory and hated defeat; her entire purpose as a cheerleader was to assist in victory. But she found herself captivated by Ben. Stop this daydreaming that *he*'ll win, she ordered herself. You want him beaten. Creamed. Whipped. Stomped on. He's the captain of the opposite team, not your boyfriend!

But daydreams are not easily tossed aside. Nancy's dreams of Ben grew stronger. They were not wispy, vague dreams, either, but strong, thick, detailed ones of herself and Ben.

Like Nancy, Ben paid no attention to the cheerleaders' performance. Nor did he bother with the arguing referees and coaches. He never glanced at the hundreds of fans screaming his name.

His eyes were fixed on the scoreboard and the clock, as if he were measuring his future. His face was lean and angular. His chin was held high, so that his throat seemed exposed. His shoulders were very broad, and his Garrison T-shirt clung wetly to his chest.

Nancy shivered slightly.

Beside him all boys paled. There was no comparison. Even Donny did not compare. Donny was too ordinary-looking. Too milk-and-Oreo-cookies-looking.

Ben was unreadable. Tough.

Perhaps if I knew him well, he wouldn't be so attractive to me, she thought. But he's so aloof. So mysterious.

She yearned to know him well enough to find

out what was behind that mysterious toughness.

Around her the rest of Tarenton's Varsity Squad murmured tensely about the need to win, to cream Garrison and Ben. Nancy forced herself to think poorly of Ben. Be still my heart, she ordered herself.

But her heart was not still. It pounded for Ben.

Olivia Evans' family history was not a joyful one. The only child of worrying parents, she had had a heart defect at birth and undergone considerable surgery to correct it. Since first grade Olivia had been fine, but her mother could not yet believe it. Mrs. Evans had wrapped herself around Olivia, protecting, coddling, and smothering.

Olivia was on speaking terms with her mother, but just barely. No sooner would she fling her mother off her back than some upsetting situation would arise and Mrs. Evans would return, clinging and clasping.

For Olivia, cheerleading was the ticket to freedom. .

Cheerleading was her first experience in a tight-knit group and Angie Poletti, Mary Ellen, and Nancy were her first close girl friends. She learned to unwind and let herself go. For the first time, Olivia had fun. It was like having childhood at the wrong end of the age spectrum — as a high school sophomore instead of a second grader.

But Mrs. Evans was sure that cheerleading was a corrupting influence.

Olivia protested constantly. "We're not wicked, Mother. We're a nice bunch of kids. Truly. Nobody drinks. Nobody does drugs. Nobody steals." Her mother would mention that terrible episode with Mary Ellen. "Mother," Olivia would repeat, "Mary Ellen was set up. She did *not* shoplift. You know that. And besides, cheerleading is good for me."

Like Mary Ellen, Olivia wanted to be Number One.

Her need wasn't quite as intense. She was willing to be a member of the Number One squad, rather than being the Number One girl. Olivia regarded Donny silently, and did not want him anyhow. Mary Ellen was attracted to Donny because he was important and not because she loved him. Well, everybody knew that, and nobody seemed to mind.

Nobody except Patrick Henley. Dark, strong, loving Patrick.

It blew Olivia's mind that Mary Ellen chose Donny instead of Patrick. Patrick literally offered himself to her and Mary Ellen turned her back. Over and over this happened, all year long. Amazing that Mary Ellen preferred others; even more amazing that Patrick kept adoring her in spite of the public hurts. But Mary Ellen was not going to date a boy who drove a garbage truck, even though it was his own. She wouldn't date him, even though he attracted her more than any boy — no matter how rich or how important — had.

Right now Mary Ellen had Donny by a thread. Not the noose Patrick was on. Just a slender thread. Perhaps it was a thread of hope, but Olivia didn't think so. Donny seemed very very interested in Mary Ellen.

Olivia forgot romance when she saw Garrison cheering.

They were so good!

Traditional — very, very traditional — but *good*.

It cut her to the core to hear Tarenton fans cheering Garrison girls. She put rage out of her mind, and jealousy and hurt. She analyzed the style, the appeal, the technique.

We can't dance like that, she realized. We have to capitalize on the strengths we've got, and dancing isn't one of them.

To prevent arguments with her mother, Olivia had toned down her own gymnastic routines. Now she knew that had been the wrong tactic. If you've got it, flaunt it. And Olivia had it. Her tiny, wiry body was light enough to catapult through the air, and she had tremendous strength in her thigh muscles. She could leave the ground as if gravity did not exist. And the squad was not making use of these abilities.

We will now, she thought grimly.

* * *

15

"It is time," Mary Ellen said, sagging with exhaustion, "for rubber wallpaper."

The Varsity Squad laughed in chorus.

Walt Manners said, "*You* may need a padded cell, Mary Ellen, but I personally thrive on this sort of thing."

Walt hugged all the girls. The most easy-going boy they had ever known, Walt was everybody's boyfriend and nobody's date. For years he'd half loved Mary Ellen, which he knew was crazy, because Melon loved exclusively on the basis of rank. Donny Parrish was currently number one, and therefore Mary Ellen loved Donny.

Walt had a pretty high score, due to his parents, rather than himself. They ran their own television talk show every morning. Walt had an eternal popularity from this, but he did not have enough on his own to get Mary Ellen.

In some ways Walt didn't mind. You had girl friends, you had problems.

Tarenton had lost to Garrison by three points. Walt knew the boys' locker room would be a scene of anger, shame, and hurt. Especially for Donny, who was expected to triumph at all times. Losing to Ben would not help his status. Donny was good, but Ben was better. It would be agony for Donny to realize that. Walt had a hunch, knowing Donny as he did, that Donny would blame everyone else for the loss — not for one minute would he entertain the possibility that he wasn't as good.

And the same went for Mary Ellen. She didn't date Number Two.

"What happens now?" Angie said in a ragged voice. She was actually crying. She wanted to win so much! She had cheered so hard, cared so deeply. Never once had she taken her attention off the game, never once had she thought of anything but victory.

Angie Poletti was really the backbone of the squad. She cheered because she loved to. She was loyal and honest, and when she was on the floor she was radiant.

And in spite of her wishes — her prayers, in fact — they lost.

Pres beat Walt to the comforting hug. With Angie and Angie only, Pres Tilford was brotherly. Any other time, Pres was the stud of the school. A girl here, a girl there.

Walt grinned, shaking his head. No, all that was changed now. Pres was in love. It was the funniest thing to see. Pres head over heels in love with a chubby little nothing sophomore named Kerry Elliot.

He marveled that Pres (a ten if ever there was one) would fall for a five. A boy with wealth and social position, brains and looks, whose father owned Tarenton Fabrication, was in love with a girl who had none of those. And Walt didn't think Kerry's appeal was willing sex, either. He was ninety percent sure they weren't going all the way. They just didn't have the look of two kids

17

who knew each other that intimately. They were too dreamy. Too nervous and anxious with each other.

Walt liked Kerry. And the girls on the squad were nice to Kerry (they would not have dared be otherwise, because so much was done as a group) but they were confused by her. Kerry was so ordinary.

Pres was so special.

Walt shrugged. Love lives were other people's problems.

Nancy Goldstein was first out of the girls' locker room.

Her eyes traveled around the crowded halls, searching for her parents, but she didn't see them. Her throat was parched from all that shouting. How she would like lemonade. Not soda. Not anything carbonated. But orange juice, or lemonade. Cool and soothing.

Tarenton had vending machines in two places: the student lounge and the cafeteria corridor. It was the machine near the cafeteria that dispensed nutritious stuff: apples, boxes of raisins, beef broth, and fruit juices. Nancy walked slowly down the hall toward that one, feeling in her coat pocket for change.

The hall was dimly lit.

A red EXIT sign glowed at the far end, lending a rosy half light to the corridor. In front of her, Nancy's shadow lengthened, shivering and spreading out in dark, mystical patterns.

She was so tired. She had never cheered so hard, never struggled so much to keep a crowd from being too excited. Usually it was the squad's task to stir up excitement. Lately, it had been the reverse: keeping all that excitement in check.

She heaved a great sigh; pushing her thick, dark hair from her face; and felt marginally more alive.

In front of her, black shadows thickened and the faint light from behind was blocked out. The glimmer of the red EXIT sign shimmered ahead but cast no real light on the floor where she walked. She put out hesitant fingers and found the wall surface. Like a blind person she moved ahead.

There was a slithering sound behind her, and a creak.

Nancy's skin crawled.

She was completely removed from the chaos of the emptying school. As isolated as if she were down some dark, deserted alley. Once she turned this corner she would be out of sight and sound of everybody.

The body heat of overwork faded. Her palms grew damp.

This is ridiculous, she thought. This is ordinary, old Tarenton High. What am I afraid of? My locker is only fifty feet from here.

The darkness was complete.

It was as if doors had been shut on her, trapping her in dusty silence. Unmistakably she heard the soft, sinister sound of a person sneaking up on her. Terrified, Nancy whirled.

A pair of ghostly hands rose in her face.

Nancy tried to scream, but nothing came from her exhausted throat except a gurgle of fear.

No! she thought. *Oh, my God, no!*

CHAPTER

"I'm sorry. I'm *really* sorry. Don't have a heart attack," said a voice.

The body towered over her. Nancy sincerely tried not to have a heart attack. Her hands, up in front of her to protect herself, were caught by the hands of the man facing her.

"It's only me," he said.

"Only who?" she whispered. She was shivering with cold fear. What did I think he was going to do? she wondered.

"Ben Adamson," he said, and now she could make him out dimly: the hawk features, the bony lines. "I'm just getting orange juice from that vending machine. Isn't it back here some-where? I can't quite remember from last year."

"You took two decades off my life," Nancy said furiously. "Creeping up on me like that! Do you realize I am now old enough to be your mother?"

Ben began laughing.

Nancy had never heard him laugh. In fact, she had not thought of him as the sort of person who knew *how* to laugh. She would have said Ben was too tough for laughter. He might glare, or snarl, but never laugh.

"You look familiar," Ben said, squinting at her.

He came from a very large high school. Probably one reason for the vicious rivalry was that Garrison had twice as many kids as Tarenton, and Garrison absolutely hated being beaten by the little guy.

At least I know he watched me cheer, she thought. Otherwise I wouldn't look familiar to him.

She was consumed with pleasure. Even if Ben didn't know it, his eyes had been drawn to Nancy Goldstein, just as hers had been drawn to him.

She took his hands in hers and lowered them to a more comfortable position. His fingers closed in that possessive, tough way he used throughout his life. She let him. She said, "You'd recognize me if I were wearing scarlet and white. I'm on the Tarenton cheerleading squad."

"Oh, no," said Ben and this time he grinned. In the darkness his teeth shone whitely. "I shouldn't be associating with a member of the opposite team."

"I have redeeming characteristics," Nancy said.

"You sure do." His voice was blatantly sexual. He was looking down, not at her face, but at her figure. It was the kind of thing her mother would hate. Normally Nancy would agree that she was not merely a sexual object. But Ben attracted her as no one had ever done, and she found herself posturing for him. With tacit cooperation, they moved on down the dark hall together, hands still touching, bodies apart, and turned the corner into utter darkness.

"We're never going to find the vending machine now," Ben said.

"We'll find it by the touch and feel system," Nancy said, leading him on.

Ben laughed deep in his throat. "That's my favorite system, anyhow."

It was a provocative remark. Nancy let the conversation continue in a flippant, sexual way. She could almost feel her mother standing there, eyes closed in distress. Nancy, Nancy, don't encourage this.

But she encouraged it.

He was Ben. The hawk of the opposite team.

They had reached the vending machine. "We'll have to guess at what we're taking," she said. "I think orange juice is on the far right. Press this." She held his fingers over a flat plastic square.

23

From his other hand she fished his change. The two quarters dropped into the vending machine with a muted thunk. A cup slithered down the chute and liquid whooshed into it.

"I just hope it isn't bouillon," Ben said. "What's your name, anyway?"

"Nancy Goldstein."

Ben's fingers released hers and swept over the vending machine, trying to find the opening where his drink would be sitting. Put your arms around me, she thought. But he didn't.

"It *is* orange juice," said Ben gratefully. "What a woman."

She got her own drink, moving her fingers over to the second button, and again her guess was right. The first sip was cool, sweet, tangy lemonade. Just right.

Very slowly, so as not to trip or spill their hard-won drinks, they moved back to the EXIT sign. When they turned the corner there was only the same dim light as before, but it felt like sunrise. They walked without talking to the front foyer where parents and fans still stood in knots. Policemen circulated, more relaxed than they had been an hour earlier, when they expected war to break out, but still on the lookout for sore losers or gloating victors.

Just as the two opposing basketball teams emerged from different dressing rooms, just as each boy schooled himself to remember his athletic manners, Ben and Nancy emerged from the darkness.

Ben: the boy who carried Garrison to its win.

Nancy: the girl who was supposed to cheer Tarenton to *its* win.

What a pair they made. Her lovely dark hair and narrow shoulders were framed against his huge body. Both protected themselves from the sudden light by looking sideways at each other.

The face of every single Tarenton basketball player tightened. Nancy Goldstein. *Their* cheerleader? Sneaking off into the dark to neck with the captain of the opposite team?

Smirks appeared on the faces of the Garrison boys. Not only could Ben steal the game from Tarenton — he could also steal the girls.

"Way to go, Ben," the co-captain said. "I like it when a victory is really complete."

Ben grinned arrogantly. You knew that Ben never settled for less than a complete victory. His eyes moved slowly across the foyer until they met Donny's, and Ben grinned even more widely. The hand that held the orange juice cup casually flicked it across the floor to the trash can. He didn't miss that basket any more than he had missed during the game. He put his hand on Nancy's shoulder.

Possessively.

The way he had owned the game, he seemed to own Nancy.

Cops and parents felt the instant furious change in atmosphere and moved uncertainly to stop things — but they weren't sure what they should be stopping.

The Tarenton Varsity Cheerleading Squad stared at their sixth member with horror and rage.

The Garrison Varsity Cheerleading Squad giggled. Their co-captain said, "Now Ben. Give poor old Tarenton a break. Let them keep *something* for themselves."

Nancy loathed scenes. She could not believe she was the center of one. Dozens of hostile eyes bored into her, silently calling her traitor.

But nothing happened! she thought. They have no right to look at me like that.

Ben Adamson loved a scene. Being the center of a fight was his life. For him, basketball was a fight, and later on in the year baseball would be another fight. He would never pass up a chance to start trouble.

Too much an actor to smile outwardly, Ben smiled inwardly. With his darkest expression, profile at its most hawklike, he said, "Saturday night, Nancy?"

She stared up at him.

"Good," he said. He leaned over — quite a distance, because Nancy was not tall — and kissed her mouth. Slowly, lingeringly.

There was an audible gasp from the Tarenton kids.

Nancy blushed.

People drew conclusions from the blush that would have shocked Nancy. Ben, satisfied by the hot red cheeks looking up at him, said calmly, "Seven-thirty." He thought, Look her up in the phone book. There can't be that many Goldsteins. Give her a call. She'll go. They all do.

He sauntered away from her to join his team. When he led the way to the team bus, he did not look back.

The Tarenton Wolves and the Tarenton Varsity Squad stared at Nancy Goldstein. She had no idea what to say to them. She couldn't begin to think. And she was furious that she had to say anything. It was all crazy! It —

"Nancy, it's time to go home.. We've been looking for you everywhere," her father said. His voice was scratchy and tired. Any other time she would have realized it was because he'd been cheering himself. Good news, when her father considered cheerleading the lowest possible activity for a liberated young girl.

But tonight she did not care whether he approved of cheerleading or not. She could think only of that kiss. A kiss she had never expected. Did not understand. Had no idea how to deal with.

Saturday night? she thought. Seven-thirty? Was he kidding?

A Tarenton girl muttered, "You couldn't find her because she was off making time with the enemy."

27

"I was not!" Nancy cried.

"At least don't be a hypocrite," Mary Ellen said coldly. "If you're going to be a traitor, admit it. That's the American tradition, isn't it? Benedict Arnold...."

Her parents, who were paying no attention to this whatsoever, dragged her off to the car. The silent, angry stares of the kids Nancy cared about most pierced her back.

Too late now to laugh it off.

Too late to giggle and say, "Adamson, go drink your orange juice and stop bothering me."

Tomorrow there would be an important and very long practice. Mary Ellen and Olivia were determined to learn routines so impressive the world would fall off its axis. And when she, Nancy, walked in, they'd snarl at her. Because they thought she'd been necking with the captain of the opposite team.

I wish, Nancy thought, forgetting everything but the possibility of Saturday night.

Donny left Tarenton High without going near Mary Ellen.

Mary Ellen pretended that this was reasonable. She pretended that, given the shock of his loss, the exhaustion of such a long, difficult game, Donny had a right to slouch on home alone.

But *oh*, how she had counted on this evening!

She had seen them in the pizza parlor where

28

everybody went after a victory: laughter bubbling like the soda they poured from huge, cold pitchers, romance blooming like the artificial flowers that sat in the middle of the scarred tables beside the thick, sputtering candles.

Mary Ellen and Donny.

Number One and Number One.

She had wanted to hold Donny, and be held by him.

She wanted to see Donny, and be seen in his company.

And loss had ended that.

Angie — sweet gentle Angie — said, "It seems to me Donny shouldn't sulk. So we lost. He did his best. Why can't he come for pizza anyway? He's not acting his age."

"It wasn't his fault," Mary Ellen said fiercely. "It was —" she could never say that it was because Ben was better — "it was stupid referees."

"Even so," Angie said, "I don't like people who sulk. And Donny's sulking."

"The final touch was Nancy," Olivia said. "Could you *believe* Nancy, our *Nancy*, making time with Ben? Thirty seconds after we lose to them?"

Mary Ellen turned her anger to Nancy. Much easier, much more convenient to dislike Nancy instead of Donny. She went for pizza with the others and they spent much of the time saying terrible things about Nancy.

"Stop," Kerry said. "Stop it now. I can't stand it."

They all stared at her.

Kerry marveled at the courage she had gotten from dating Pres. She — dull, little nothing sophomore Kerry — could sit here and talk back to these shining stars: to Mary Ellen and Angie and the rest. She said, "So Nancy has a new boyfriend. We don't have to be spiteful."

The rest were silenced, considering. Nancy *was* their friend and fellow cheerleader.

After a while Mary Ellen said, "Still and all, if Nancy were to come down with a disfiguring disease, I wouldn't go hunting for the cure."

They giggled.

Pres, who was ready at any time to make wisecracks at anyone's expense, loved Kerry again for being nice.

Mary Ellen, for whom being nice sometimes took real effort, struggled to shrug about Nancy. She had never been able to shrug about any defeat. She did not see how she could shrug about this one. But they all had to work together the next day, and Nancy was as important to the squad as any other member.

Other people are naturally good, she thought. Look at Kerry. She really meant that. She really doesn't have any hard feelings. Me, I have to *coach* myself to be good. I have to memorize the *rules* in order to be good.

Five of the six Varsity members were having pizza. It was a loss not to have Nancy. We're a squad, Mary Ellen reminded herself. And I'm the captain. The squad comes first. I won't be angry with Nancy. No matter how much she deserves it.

CHAPTER

Nancy Goldstein missed the school bus, and ran down to the corner to flag a ride with her neighbor, only to see the car disappear around the bend. Oh, no! I can't be late, she thought. We've got that exam first period.

She ran home again, her books a dead weight in her arms, and raced in the door screaming, "Mom! Mom!"

Her mother, looking lovely in a cranberry red suit with a paisley-patterned silk blouse, was just slipping on a pair of shoes.

"Missed the bus, Mother. Can you drive me?"

Mrs. Goldstein glared at her daughter. "Honestly, Nancy. You've been up for an hour. How could you have possibly missed that bus? You know I work this morning. I don't have time to drive you."

Nancy had dawdled because of daydreams. Ben. The texture of the hands she had so briefly touched. The profile in the dim hall, the slight pressure of his unexpected kiss.

Wondering, over and over — did he mean it about Saturday? Do I want to have him mean it? What will it be like in school if I actually *do* date Ben Adamson?

"Mother, please? I have an exam first class. I've got to get there on time. I'm really, really sorry. Please drive me?"

Mrs. Goldstein gave in. She always did. She wanted to be stern and unyielding because it sounded like such a good way to parent, but Nancy was such a good daughter and a fine student that it was hard. Besides, they lived so far from Tarenton High it would take Nancy hours to walk there.

"All right, all right. Hurry up." Mrs. Goldstein reached for her coat and keys. They drove fast, Nancy's mother peering at her watch and worrying about being late herself. She was teaching an art history class in Garrison, and gave stern remarks to students who were late. She dreaded the thought of being late herself.

" 'Bye, Mom," Nancy said, leaping out of the car. She shouted thank you over her shoulder, but Mrs. Goldstein was already driving off.

Nancy ran into the huge lobby, her shoes clicking on the marble floor.

Nancy loved going into Tarenton High. Its design was a combination of formality and coziness that made her want to write to the long-dead architect and congratulate him. Just walking in was a good feeling. And it wasn't often that you felt that way about your school.

Except for a few kids rushing to homeroom late, the lobby was empty. A grundgy boy Nancy didn't know looked hard at her. "Oh. It's the little rah-rah," he said nastily. His voice frightened her. It was savage. Like a piece of violence left over from the game. "You having a good time being rotten, Goldstein?"

Nancy stopped walking, as stunned as if he'd hit her. Being rotten?

"Real wholesome bunch, you cheerleaders. Running around making time with the opposition. I like it, Goldstein. I really like it." He flicked a dirty sweatshirt in her direction. A sick taste rose in her mouth. Oh, please, no! she thought. Please don't let anybody else feel that way.

The boy left her alone. She walked unsteadily to her locker, down the very same hall she had last walked with Ben. Her palms were wet with apprehension. Was this how the whole school would react?

Taped to her locker was a little piece of paper. When Nancy read the words, she gasped and jumped backward, her hand over her mouth, her books cascading to the floor unnoticed. *Nobody would call me that! That's meant for someone else.*

She could scarcely bring herself to touch the locker, but she had to put her coat in and get out another notebook. Standing to the side, as if the horrid lettering could touch her, Nancy managed to retrieve her book. Ripping the paper off made her gag. She scrunched it up and threw it in the bottom of her locker. She'd throw it away somewhere else when she wasn't so upset. And didn't have an exam in ten seconds.

Who would write something like that? Vanessa? She *would* think being the daughter of the superintendent of schools would give her the right to do anything. But even Vanessa wouldn't print anything that ugly.

Running again, Nancy tried to fix her mind on advanced English literature. Never had this been so difficult.

She walked into class late. Being late always meant a brief flicker of embarrassment as eyes turned to assess the latecomer, but this time the thirty pairs of eyes seemed sharply judgmental. Nancy slid into a vacant seat at the back next to Mary Ellen. Melon, her friend and co-cheerleader, did not look at her.

Mary Ellen took every opportunity to smile. She had the finest teeth, the loveliest lips, and the fairest complexion in Tarenton, and she liked to show off the combination in a welcoming smile.

But she didn't even look up to greet Nancy.

Nobody looked up to greet Nancy.

She felt a chill as strong as if she'd walked into a restaurant freezer, and turned around to find no handle to get out by.

Misery engulfed Nancy. She had trouble with the test. She, who never had problems with anything printed. How she wanted everyone to like her! She had had to try so hard to win friends when she moved to Tarenton, and getting on the squad had seemed to solve it. Could she have ruined everything by something as silly as helping Ben get a cup of juice?

During passing period, she walked alone. Several people made remarks about Nancy dating the enemy. Several people made obscene gestures and one boy blocked her path threateningly. Nancy did not know what he might have done if Mrs. Oetjen, the principal, hadn't materialized at that moment.

It brought home to Nancy the enormity of the war between Tarenton and Garrison. This year people weren't kidding. It wasn't merely basketball. It was a battle. There *must* be victory. They *must* be Number One.

They were willing to spill blood to achieve it.

My blood? she thought.

The day passed without a single encouraging

word from anybody. Nancy fled to cheerleading practice and the five companions who had to work with her, and had to smile, because that's what cheerleading was — happy enthusiasm on the move.

Forty feet from the other five, Olivia stood for one moment in motionless preparation, gathering her muscles, planning her leap. She was clad in practice clothing: sweat shorts and a T-shirt that said *Cheerleaders make better lovers*. She had never tested the validity of this, but she liked pretending she knew the score.

She was shiny with perspiration. Her light-brown, fine hair clung limply to her forehead. Olivia was totally unaware of her looks at this moment. If someone had held up a mirror, she would not have seen the mirror, let alone the reflection of herself.

She was preparing to do the most daring jump she had ever attempted.

Pres Tilford stood tensely. He was sure of Olivia and he was sure of himself, but they had never practiced this. There was no way to rehearse, according to Olivia. They would start with the real thing. Nerves prickled on the back of his neck and the palms of his hands. The hands were cupped. He had taken off his ring.

Olivia drew herself together abruptly and began to run. Her remarkably strong legs and thighs propelled her along the gym floor at an astounding rate. It did not seem possible that she could achieve such a speed in such a short distance. Like an Olympic champion, Olivia leaped into the air, her right foot landing squarely in Pres's cupped hands. Pres thrust upward, adding height to her speed, and Olivia's slender, fragile body flew into the air.

The other four cheerleaders, lined up behind Pres, lifted their arms in a series of rotating fluid motions, as if they were tossing Olivia like feathers into the sky. Above their fingers, Olivia somersaulted, spread her legs, touched her toes, and landed perfectly: feet together, back arched, small breasts lifted, narrow waist in. She neither stumbled nor clutched the air, but simply stood there, as if she had strolled over to that position.

Mrs. Engborg, the coach, closed her eyes with relief.

If Olivia landed neck first from such a height at such a speed. . . . But it was better not to think of such things.

Ardith Engborg had never seen her squad like this. In all the years she had coached cheerleading, she'd never run into a year of such determination, such icy fury. The rivalry against Garrison had reached such proportions that even the cheerleading squads were pitted against each other.

Mary Ellen and Olivia had proclaimed that

the next time they appeared in public, they would be so spectacular that the entire gym would gasp when they performed. And perform they would. Not cheer. Not chant. Not clap. *Perform.*

"Olivia," Ardith Engborg said quietly, "that was magnificent."

Olivia nodded. She had that knowledge of her own ability that goes with being a truly fine athlete. Nervous, yes. Willing to practice for hours, yes. But confident. She *knew* she was good. She knew she was magnificent.

Pres Tilford thought, What if she'd missed my hands? What if I lifted too hard, and threw her to the side, or didn't lift enough and —

He stopped his thoughts.

Pres disliked thinking of failure. Success was everything to Pres. In some ways Pres was very much like his wealthy, social parents — he could not bear to be associated with anything or anyone but a winner.

Olivia's a winner, he thought, watching her objectively. He admired Olivia immensely, but his eyes went to the bleachers, where Kerry, whom he loved, sat with Patrick. The admirers: Kerry of Pres, Patrick of Mary Ellen. But Kerry did not have to admire from afar. Pres would gladly take her in his arms.

But Ardith pulled them back for the demonstration of a cheer Mary Ellen had devised. It was a very complex leap-frog maneuver. They flung themselves over each other's backs in a whipping tempo that would result in broken ribs for those whose timing was off.

When they finished that, they collapsed on the floor, gasping for air, passing the water bottle around and sucking eagerly on the clear plastic straw.

Angie said tentatively, "You know, these cheers are impressive, but they're not really *cheers*. This is like a gymnastics meet."

Mary Ellen was in no mood for dissension. "It'll make us Number One," she said flatly.

"But do we really want to be Number One?" Angie said wistfully. "I kind of like the old cheers. Clapping and shifting feet and . . . you know . . . plain old rhythms that everybody knows."

They stared at her as if tradition was a sin.

"Angie, those old cheers didn't get us anywhere," Olivia said. Olivia was incensed that Angie was not one hundred percent thrilled by her performance.

"They've gotten us championships for years," Angie pointed out.

"But this is not an ordinary year!" Olivia cried. "Don't you understand that Garrison is trying to whip us? They have that Ben Adamson" — she spoke his name like a curse — "and Ben might actually outplay Donny."

"Impossible," Mary Ellen said sharply. She had stayed up last night, hoping that Donny would call. Suggest a movie, a drive, a meal together. Talk about the game, about future games. But he had not called. She had no way of knowing if she had just been a passing fancy, or if he was just too busy or too hurt to do anything right now.

Her eyes went to Nancy at the mention of Ben Adamson, but Mary Ellen wrenched her thoughts away from that pair. She had promised herself not to think bad thoughts. Instead she looked up into the bleachers. Kerry and Patrick. She possessed Patrick. She knew it. But she didn't want Patrick. She wanted Donny. No, that wasn't true. She did want Patrick. If he had been Number One in anything, she would have loved him forever. As it was, in her most honest moments, face to face with herself, she knew she loved Patrick in a way she never had loved any other boy. She just wouldn't let the world know it . . . or Patrick.

Nancy decided to say nothing. Nothing had happened with Ben, despite what it had looked like, and she didn't know if anything would. Leave it alone.

But that was not anyone else's decision. Angie burst out, her school loyalty superceding her sweetness, "Nancy, how *could* you? I think the least a person loyal to Tarenton could do is to wait until after basketball season. Is that so much to ask? A cheerleader of *all* people shouldn't display a lack of loyalty in public."

Five sets of eyes bored into Nancy.

"Look," she said, trying not to cry, "Ben is

41

just a show-off. It was nothing. Nothing. I don't even know him."

They were uniformly skeptical.

"Really," she protested. "We were just going down the hall for lemonade and it was dark so we walked together."

"What were you doing in a dark hall all alone?" Angie asked. "I mean, when *I'm* with a terrific boy all alone in a dark hall —"

"He is *not* a terrific boy," Mary Ellen said fiercely. "He looks like a criminal. He probably pushes drugs. Steals cars. He's a creep."

"He is not!" Nancy cried. "You're just making that up. You're just jealous."

Immediately she knew she had made a terrible error.

Not only would the rest think she had a boyfriend to defend, but she had accused Mary Ellen of jealousy, saying without meaning to that Ben was better than Donny.

"Whether he's a creep or a teddy bear," Olivia said, "right now he's the enemy and I think it's pretty low of you to associate with him, Nancy."

I won't lose my temper. I won't cry, Nancy told herself. I'll get out of this and we'll all still be friends. "I'm not associating with him. I don't even know him. He was just there."

"Oh. That big kiss was brotherly?" Olivia snorted.

Walt Manners stood up, dusting himself off. "Listen, we've got to work on that cheer again," he said in a sparkling, cheerleader sort of voice. "Let's go, squad."

"Shut up, Walt," Olivia said.

"Now, listen," Walt protested.

"*You* listen," Olivia said. "I want to win. I don't care about anything but winning. And if I have to be a one-man band, I'm going to win. I'm going to show Garrison up so much they'll be laughed off the floor. We're going to put on the best display that Tarenton has ever seen." She was on her feet now, all five feet one inch of her, and her tiny foot stomped with a strength that proved her athletic ability, like a piston on an engine.

Walt shrugged. He detested arguments. He looked at Angie, who had not really meant to start anything. They all stood, ready to work again, letting the subject drop, letting Mary Ellen and Olivia run the show as they chose.

Pres steered clear of the whole thing. From this distance Kerry looked faintly blurry. She was a fluffy sort of girl anyway, with her hair ruffled and out of place, her soft collars and pink mohair sweaters adding to the look of fragility.

To Pres, she was exquisite.

He wanted to quit cheering and run over to her. Bound up the bleachers three at a time, fling Kerry into the air instead of Olivia, end with a passionate kiss instead of a cheer.

He could do that to Vanessa — dramatic, dark, violent Vanessa. Vanessa would have loved it, he would have loved it, the sparse audience would have loved it.

But Kerry was shy.

Much as she loved being seen in Pres's company, she did not like having attention drawn to her. She would hate that sort of trick on his part.

For Kerry's sake, Pres was revising his entire standard of behavior. Oddly enough, it wasn't hard. He had heard that personalities didn't change, but his was. Even his parents had commented on it. They were suspicious, to say the least, partly because Kerry was not what his mother had had in mind for her son's girl.

Kerry was too soft. Too quiet. Too unnoticeable.

Pres's mother was the most organized, elegant, impressive woman in Tarenton. A frequent guest on the Manners' talk show, Felicia Tilford was sharp enough to cut paper.

Pres did not want her cutting Kerry.

The squad began practicing again. It was an almost violent cheer. Angie stifled her complaints, although she wanted an entirely different kind of routine. But when Olivia did another dazzling gymnastic trick, complete with a circle of back flips and a breathtaking leap from Walt's shoulders to the floor, and off Nancy's back onto Pres's shoulders, Angie spoke up. "Cheerleaders lead cheers," she cried. "They don't perform suicidal leaps and —"

"It isn't suicidal," Olivia said. "Don't say that

word again. If my mother thought I was doing something suicidal she'd haul me out of the squad."

"She'd haul you out of the *state*," Walt said.

"Stop your chatter," Ardith Engborg said, "and *work*."

CHAPTER

They were always getting an audience, as if if they were an episode on a favorite afternoon soap opera. Kids drifted in, observed the cheer-leading practice with half their attention, gos-siped softly from the upper corner of the bleach-ers, and later drifted out. As long as they were relatively quiet, Mrs. Engborg never complained. The cheerleaders tried harder when they were being watched, and it helped condition them to an audience.

In fact the Varsity Squad had gotten so used to the quiet traffic of kids waiting for late buses, parents, or friends, that they rarely glanced at the bleachers.

But when Donny Parrish walked in, things

were different and Donny knew it. Swaggering slightly, he walked slower than he had a year before, demanding attention even as he got attention without demanding it.

Even Ardith Engborg paused to admire the boy who was Tarenton's primary hope.

As for Mary Ellen Kirkwood, her heart stopped. Hot as she was from exercise, she felt a chill. Gravely, Donny saluted her. Not a wave, not a grin, but a serious martial salute.

He came here to see me, she thought, and all the confidence she had lost returned. She had a lovely smile and she knew it. As she smiled at Donny, she lifted her scarlet pompon, swirling it in a long, slow half circle around herself. Donny smiled back. Pure joy filled Mary Ellen. She could look even at Nancy with love. All was right with the world.

Donny Parrish had come into the gymnasium to see *her*, Mary Ellen Kirkwood.

Donny climbed the bleachers and sat down beside Patrick. Mary Ellen tried to ignore Patrick. On Donny's other side was Kerry. At last Mary Ellen had found something worthwhile in Kerry — no competition.

A wisp of understanding passed briefly through her mind. Perhaps Pres Tilford adored Kerry *because* she was no competition. But as soon as Mary Ellen had the idea, she forgot it. Donny consumed her, mind and body.

* * *

Only a month earlier, Kerry would have been destroyed by Donny's presence. Her tongue would have failed her. Her hands would have betrayed her, trembling and fidgeting. She would have lurched around, embarrassed, unable to cope with the presence of the star of the high school. She — a lowly, chubby sophomore — in the company of Donny Parrish.

But being Pres's girl had changed her more than she knew.

Pres impressed her so much that another boy could not impress her more. Sure, Donny was a high-scoring basketball player, but big deal. Look at all that her Pres was!

So she smiled comfortably at Donny. "Hi, there," she said. "The squad is coming up with some unbelievable new routines. You'll be amazed at what Olivia Evans can do. She's absolutely wonderful."

Donny nodded. "Actually," he said, "I came to watch Mary Ellen."

Kerry ached with happiness for Mary Ellen. She would quote Donny, and Mary Ellen would bask in the words. Kerry ached equally with pain for Patrick. She moved a little, to block Patrick from Donny, to give him a little privacy so he could absorb the rivalry without being watched.

Patrick leaned forward and watched Mary Ellen — the golden hair and long legs. He knew a lot about her. How she felt in his arms; how her mouth felt under his; and how she sighed when he kissed her. He knew she would come and go, but he could wait. He had something Mary Ellen always came back to. He counted on it.

I know how you feel, Patrick, Kerry thought. You're competing with the star. We all know which one Mary Ellen will choose.

She glanced at Patrick.

He smiled back.

"Life can be a pain," Kerry said to him.

"Agreed."

He knew she understood, and welcomed the understanding. No need for more words on such a painful topic.

Oh, Pres, thought Kerry. If what is between you and me were to end tonight, I've learned so much. I've learned to love. To be friendlier. To care more, enjoy more. Life is so much more intense than it was before I fell in love with you.

So much emotion in this room, she thought. So many of us tangled up with feelings we can't entirely deal with.

On the floor, Olivia and Pres went through their hurling routine again. Kerry quivered with fear as Olivia went so dangerously high above the ground. Her little body came down with such force! If they mistimed. . . .

"Wow," Donny said softly. "That's some leap."

The squad repeated the routine, and this time the sparse audience, perhaps a dozen at the moment, burst into applause. Impossible not to acknowledge the brilliance — the daring, dazzling brilliance — that Olivia displayed. Olivia turned to face them, an expression of triumph on her face.

This would wipe Garrison's squad off the map, and she knew it.

She thrust her arms up in a victorious jabbing motion that cut the air. The audience clapped harder.

"Two stars," Kerry commented. "You, Donny. And now Olivia."

Donny smiled. It was a quiet smile, but she knew that he loved being called a star. Who wouldn't, after all?

Patrick and Donny began talking casually about the yearbook, and the informal pictures now being taken. Donny was afraid the basketball team would get short shrift. Patrick assured Donny that the basketball team was the *last* group to get shafted.

"Shrifted, you mean," Donny said.

They argued about whether it was shafted, or shrifted. But they both knew they were arguing about Mary Ellen, vying for her.

And into the gymnasium came Ben Adamson.

Hulking, dark, beaky as Pike's Peak. Shoulders moving in opposing directions, as if he had enough muscle for two normal people.

The cheerleaders decorated the floor like so many cookies and glasses of milk. Pure wholesomeness. Clean-cut, all-round American youth.

Sweet smiles, happy gestures, pure thoughts. (Or so it looked.)

Ben. He truly looked like a criminal.

And he was. The most wanted criminal on the Tarenton High list.

It was unthinkable that Ben would saunter into their gym at a time when feelings were so high. All very well to say they were mature high school students who could handle their negative emotions — but they weren't . . . and they couldn't.

Ben was asking for a fight.

With Ben standing there, as if hewn from rock — granite — it was impossible to remember the existence of Donny Parrish. What was Donny but some guy sprawled on the top bleacher? Ben possessed the gymnasium floor like an explorer, the wilderness.

Donny knew it, and hated Ben Adamson.

Ben. Here. In his gym. On his turf.

I'll kill him in the next game, Donny thought. I'll plaster him to the walls. I'll destroy him.

But Ben never glanced his way. In that infuriating arrogant manner that so far surpassed Donny's own — because it was natural and Donny had *taught* himself how to be arrogant — Ben dominated the entire room.

The cheerleaders faltered and stared at Ben. Even when Donny had come into the gym, practice had not stopped, merely paused for a few seconds of recognition.

It's that worthless Nancy Goldstein, thought

Donny. He's actually come here, to my gym, to pick her up. They probably have some hot date somewhere. He turned his hatred equally on Nancy.

Ben's chin lifted fractionally. His cold stare sliced the atmosphere of the gym. The chin lifted to greet Nancy, and they all knew it.

Ardith Engborg cleared her throat noisily. "Squad," she said, "we'll work on the halftime show now, please."

She put the tape on. Blasting, pounding, throbbing rock music filled the large gym. The Varsity Squad spread out to begin an equally pounding, throbbing display.

Donny was blinded by rage. He could not even see Mary Ellen, gracefully taking center front. He thought, I'd like to see Ben take an icy curve too fast in the dark. Donny's jacket brushed Kerry's.

It seemed to Kerry she could feel his hatred right through the fabric. She sent Patrick a panicky look. Right now, because someone can toss little balls into a net a little better, Donny would probably kill.

She shuddered. Donny was unaware of her existence, let alone her shudder.

As for Patrick Henley, he felt the burden of a sense of duty. Whether it was duty to Mary Ellen or to Tarenton High, he did not know. He also had a maturity the others didn't have. Maybe it was because he had worked hard to get what he wanted . . . his own truck. And next came Mary Ellen. He wanted her, too.

The girl he adored did not love him back. It was a terrible, painful nuisance. If he could have tossed his feelings for Mary Ellen aside, he would have done so immediately. Odd how easy it was to toss physical objects. Patrick, who owned his own garbage truck and had his own lucrative route in Tarenton, did more of that than any kid in the county. But emotions could not be tossed so readily. They had lives of their own.

He watched Mary Ellen now. Saw her slip, and mess up part of the routine because she was watching Donny, watching Ben, divided by a tumult of emotions that she could not control, any more than he could control his love for her.

Kerry murmured, "Patrick, what'll we do? Donny's going to explode. If he starts a fight, he'll be thrown off the team. And then we'll lose everything."

At last Ben glanced at them. His expressionless eyes met the smoldering hatred in Donny's eyes. And Ben was amused. He smiled at Donny, as if Donny were a child to be toyed with. Donny stood up, fists bunched.

Nancy was very, very grateful for all the hours of hard practice that had come before today. If she had not known her routines so thoroughly, she could never have kept going under the iron gaze of Ben Adamson.

For me, she thought, stunned. He's here for me. There can't be any other reason. *He can't wait until Saturday and he's come for me now*!

But what should she do? Walk over after practice ends? Hug him? Beam with pleasure? Pretend dismay that he'd interrupted an important practice?

But the only emotion to grip her was the thrill of being wanted. She didn't care how presumptuous Ben was.

It was like being wanted by a god. Lesser mortals would have to stand aside.

Patrick was not as tall as Ben — nobody was — but in his own way he, too, commanded attention. Ben had been designed for arrogance and game-playing, but Patrick was broader, and more real, and tougher beneath the surface than any of them.

With an easy grin, easy speech, easy manner, Patrick walked Ben off the floor and sat him down on the bottom bleacher in a less threatening posture. When Nancy joined them, twenty minutes later, Patrick escorted them to the door, blocking the astonished teenagers who wouldn't dare tangle with Patrick any more than with Ben.

My good deed for the day, Patrick thought wryly.

Saint, he told himself cynically.

He looked across the floor and his dark eyes met Mary Ellen's blues ones. She smiled at Patrick, a shy, odd smile for Mary Ellen. He never failed her, she couldn't help thinking. Patrick was always there for her. Their eyes clung and then Mary Ellen looked away.

Ardith Engborg watched the procession leaving the gym. She was no less astounded than the students that Ben Adamson had come to Tarenton to get Nancy. Ardith did not know Ben at all, but she knew one thing: Ben had not shown up because of a deep, abiding love for Nancy. He had shown up in order to show off.

That boy's name isn't Ben, thought the coach. It's Trouble.

CHAPTER 5

Kerry was knitting a sweater for Pres. Lopi wool: fat thick lambswool in undyed colors of deep brown, soft fisherman's ivory, and misty grey. It worked up quickly because the yarn was so fat and the circular needles so large. Kerry had never knit anything in the round before, and it was so easy. She could not imagine why anybody ever knit a sweater in four pieces when you could make it like this.

Pres did not know about the sweater. It was a surprise for his birthday. Sometimes Kerry daydreamed about that day. His parents would do something spectacular, she knew. And she would be a central part of it.

Out on the court Pres was wearing a torn pair

of gym shorts and an old torn T-shirt in sweatshirt grey. His socks had no elastic left and his toes showed through the ripped sneakers. You would not have known that Pres could buy and sell every person in the gym.

Or, at least, his father could. Pres was on a slim allowance. His father said if Pres wanted more money, he could earn it at Tarenton Fabricators, working the loading dock. But Pres hated the thought of this and simply went without instead. Kerry actually had more spending money than the wealthy Pres!

She forget Ben as soon as Patrick seated him. For Kerry there was no male human being but Pres.

Even after weeks of dating Pres, Kerry felt flippy floppy when he talked to her. She still got flustered when he blew her a kiss in the halls, and tongue-tied when a knot of senior boys with Pres in the center stopped to talk to her for a few moments.

She knew they thought she was an odd choice. She knew they wondered just what there was about her that attracted Pres. What if, one dismal morning, Pres wondered that himself?

One reason Kerry had not told Pres about the sweater was her fear that he'd break up with her before his birthday and she'd never have a chance to give it to him. She hadn't even told her parents that the sweater was for Pres!

Icelandic sweaters were unisex. You just decided the chest size and started knitting. It was an outdoor sweater, meant to be worn over lots of clothing. She had a brother and a father who could enjoy the sweater, and she knew they half expected to be getting it themselves.

Every night that she wasn't out with Pres, Kerry stayed home, did her homework, and then went to the living room to watch TV and knit. She sat in the old wing chair, its upholstery half worn to threads where elbows and cats' claws had worked it over. Such a comfortable old chair. Perfect to curl up in with a long-term project.

And certainly a sweater was a long-term project. Kerry had never before known a boy she would have knit for. Knitting took hours and hours, night after night, week after week. You didn't knit a sweater for a boy unless you really and truly loved him.

She watched Pres cheer. Oh, Pres, I love you! she thought with delight and fear.

The practice ended. Everybody's attention followed the peculiar trio of Ben, Nancy, and Patrick out the door. Everybody's except Kerry's. Eyes glued to Pres, she walked down the bleachers — always tricky, always the fear she'd catch her ankle and trip and either kill herself (thus losing Pres forever) or make a fool of herself (she believed Pres would rather have her dead than be a fool).

Pres waved at her. "I'm too sweaty," he said.

"I'll take a shower and meet you in ten minutes, okay?"

"Okay," she said, smiling. He could do it, too. If she had to take a shower and meet him, she'd be forty-five minutes. He'd be ten. She sat on the bottom bleacher now and looked at the sweep hand on her watch, guessing exactly what he was doing every moment, imagining his body in the shower.

Wow, she thought, shaking her head to clear it. Think about knitting instead, Kerry old girl.

Pres charged into the gym, did a cartwheel over to her, and misjudged his timing, so that he skidded into her ankles and nearly knocked her skull into the wall. "Sorry about that," he said, and kissed her instead. She blushed and looked around, but there was nobody there. Pres took her arm with the eager affection that always knocked her off her feet, and they walked out into the hall and headed for the front foyer.

Pres was bouncing like a little kid.

"Where do you get all this energy?" she marveled. "You just went through the most grueling practice ever! I got so scared. Angie was right, you know. Some of Olivia's leaps really are suicidal."

Pres scoffed, in spite of the fact that he agreed. He was in a show-off mood. Usually Kerry's presence made him feel secure enough that he didn't have to show off. Today Ben's arrogance had set off a sort of eager anger: anger that any of them had been shown up, and eagerness to be sure that he still came first with Kerry.

"*Look* at that *wall*!" exclaimed Kerry. "Who on earth is *doing* all this?"

Pres looked at the wall in question.

Tarenton High had an anonymous vandal/athlete who had taken to leaving footprints on the walls. Whoever it was was agile. He could only achieve those black marks by racing up to the wall and actually running a pace or two on its vertical surface.

The unknown boy's favorite place of attack was the foyer. Flat white paint adorned its wide, high walls, and light streamed in the huge glass doors from the west-facing entrances. Tread marks were displayed to glorious advantage, and every single kid in the high school paused to admire or deplore the handiwork.

There were those who applauded every time the skidmarks appeared higher and higher on the walls.

There were those who thought it was disgusting vandalism, and helped paint over the offending black streaks each time.

Mrs. Oetjen, the principal, was out for blood. *Nothing* offended her more. Not drugs, not stealing from lockers, not academic failure, not basketball defeat. She had a thing about those white walls. The sparkling purity of that front foyer symbolized to Mrs. Oetjen a pride in learning and education. It was the first impression of the school that she ran, and she could not bear those stains.

Of course the marks didn't wash off. They were indelible, rubbery, had to be painted over, and sometimes bled through the paint, requiring another coat. Anyway, you could always tell where they'd been painted over because the paint itself made fresher, whiter streaks.

Pres said, "What do you think I should get my mother for her birthday?"

Hard to imagine beautiful Felicia Tilford getting older. Kerry doubted that the occasion was one for celebration on Felicia's part. "Well," she said, unable to think of a single item the wealthy, spoiled Felicia Tilford did not already have two of, "anybody with fingers and earlobes can always use rings and earrings."

Pres shook his head. "I've tried that. My taste is never good enough. She always tells me how *charming* they are, and how *thoughtful* I am, and then she puts the earrings back in the box and never wears them."

Kerry ached for him. Pres and his parents were endlessly getting on each other's nerves. Her own family was close in an easy, undemanding way, and she could not figure out why the three Tilfords were so irritable with each other.

"Presents are always a pain," Pres said glumly. "There was a Christmas when all I got was socks and batteries."

Kerry giggled. "Were you supposed to plug in your socks?"

"No. I guess they figured I had every battery-powered toy in the world, so all I needed were more batteries to keep them going. And I think I had so many clothes, they figured all I needed in that department was more socks."

Kerry squeezed his hand. "Bet they gave you something terrific as well. Like a Porsche."

"Nope. Got that when I turned sixteen. The year of the socks was thirteen."

They turned the corridor into the foyer. Strong sun poured in, half blinding them in the intensity of the angled setting sun. Framed like a silhouette on a white matte was a slim, dark figure with heavy black-soled shoes leaping into the air sideways, and leaving treadmarks so high they were nearly at the ceiling.

"Oh, wow!" Kerry breathed. "I hate those skidmarks, but that kid can really jump! Didn't he remind you of Olivia, leaping like that? You should have him on the cheerleading squad!"

Pres could not believe how much it hurt that Kerry thought there was somebody out there who could add to the squad. What could this kid do that he, Pres, could not do better? I'll show her! he thought. *I* can do anything, and do it *better*.

"I can leave skidmarks higher up than that," he said irritably.

"Oh, Pres, you cannot," she said.

Goaded, he left her side instantly, raced alongside the wall, gathered speed and thigh muscles, and ran up the wall. He'd never tried it before, although all the boys did it occasionally in the locker rooms, but adrenalin and the need to prove himself to Kerry won.

He didn't get any higher than the boy before him, but he equaled it. He came down, delighted with himself, out of breath, leg muscles shaking, and bumped hard into the principal's wide, unyielding bosom.

"Preston Tilford!" screamed Mrs. Oetjen, grabbing his shoulders and shaking him. She was shorter than Pres, but fury lent her strength. He stood there and let himself be shaken. "So it's *you*! I am so disgusted with you! I cannot *believe* this. This makes me *sick*, Preston Tilford! I've been on that loudspeaker every single afternoon, asking that vandal to stop ruining our beautiful school, and it's *you*!"

She released him, stepped back, and glared at him with unparalleled rage. Anything else Pres had done in his school career had been mere mischief compared to this. Mrs. Oetjen was beside herself.

In normal circumstances, Pres laughed things off. He was not given to accepting much in the way of blame, or concerning himself much over incidents that upset other people. But he had never faced such pure fury.

She was like a hurricane, ready to rip him from his foundations.

"It wasn't Pres," Kerry said quickly. "Pres didn't —"

"Kerry Elliot!" Mrs. Oejten yelled. "I just *saw* him. *You* just saw him. How *dare* you attempt to lie to protect him? I thought better of you!"

"No, no!" cried Kerry. "I'm not lying. He did do it once, but it was only once, and it was my fault. The other times he —"

"You see?" she demanded. "*The other times!*"

Kerry subsided. She was making things worse. She was a little scared by the degree of anger the principal was displaying. She had never been in any kind of trouble in her life, and she didn't want to start now.

Mrs. Oetjen said a little more quietly, "Pres, I am so disappointed in you. I thought you were calming down at last. I was impressed by how much effort you were putting into the squad. You've pulled your grades up to where they should be and your classroom behavior by and large is acceptable. Now I realize it's because you were taking out all your hostility in another way. Pres, it's one thing to take risks, which you do every time you act stupidly. But it's another to force the entire school to suffer with you. I truly believe that defacing the school, week after week, is the most anti-social act a person is capable of. Come to my office. We'll call the police first, and then your father."

CHAPTER

Nancy knew they were attracting stares. Deep down she knew they were stares of anger and hostility. But she chose not to face that. She chose to consider the attention as admiration. The raw-boned, hawk-faced young man beside her made her weak with excitement.

Patrick left them at Ben's car. She remembered to murmur good-bye, but as she slid in with Ben, all else was forgotten.

Ben drove out of the parking lot and across Tarenton just the way she expected him to: with controlled but excessive speed. He wasn't endangering lives, but he wasn't obeying the rules either.

She debated locking her seat belt. If she put

it on, she'd be safer, of course. Ben seemed the type to require a safety net. On the other hand, she'd be fastened down at greater distance from Ben than she wanted. She did not know him at all. Should she sidle over on the upholstery and sit right up next to him?

Nancy could hardly even look at him, let alone touch him. Whenever she turned his way, he also turned, his dark, piercing stare giving her more troubling thoughts than the sum total of all the other boys she had ever dated.

After three exchanges like this — no talk, just charged stares — Nancy looked out her window instead. Gas station. Parking lot. Discount shoes. I can't believe I'm looking out the window, she thought. I am sitting next to heaven, and I'm studying the billboards advertising bank interest rates.

Ben Adamson got on the bypass, more so that he could drive fast than to save time, and congratulated himself. Going to Tarenton High gymnasium had been like a battle scene without the effort a real battle would demand. He'd had a victory, but been spared the fight. Poor Donny Parrish. Good enough in a small backwater town like Tarenton, but nothing to compare with a *real* basketball player. How Ben had loved sauntering into Donny's gym, and sauntering out with little Nancy on his arm. And Nancy was so obviously thrilled about it.

Ben loved thrilling girls. And did anything he could think of to thrill them.

He took Nancy for hamburgers. She barely ate hers. Ben took this as a compliment: She was either concerned that she should not gain weight and thus be less attractive for him, or she was so nervous in his presence that she couldn't eat.

Either way suited Ben Adamson perfectly.

He thought vaguely, I'll go out with her for basketball season. Stir things up a little. It's going to be such an easy victory for me this year, this'll add a little spice to it. Then after basketball's over, maybe that new girl, Wendy.

Wendy had just moved to Garrison. Willowy, distant, shy, and graceful, she didn't look like an easy mark. Ben thought it would be fun to prove to her that she *was* easy. Ben sat over his double cheeseburger and talked to Nancy, looked at Nancy, shared the condiments with Nancy — but throughout their meal, another girl was superimposed on Nancy's face: the elusive Wendy who Ben would go after next.

"Listen," Ben said, "how about breakfast tomorrow?"

Nancy was astonished and gratified. A boy so eager to see her that he not only couldn't wait until Saturday night for their first date — he wanted to drive all the way over from Garrison early in the morning, before school, and have breakfast with her?

She said, "Oh, I'd love that, Ben." Actually Nancy never ate breakfast. Her stomach was tight and unwilling in the morning. She knew breakfast was good for you and the most important meal of the day and all that, but it had no appeal for her. If she swallowed half a glass of orange juice it was a successful morning. However, for Ben, she was even willing to face pancakes and sausage.

"The Pancake House?" she guessed, because it was the only place in Tarenton that served decent breakfasts.

Ben simply laughed and shook his head.

Immediately she felt unsophisticated and ignorant. There must be some special place she didn't know about.

Ben lifted her hand, looked at it for a long moment, and kissed each finger, running his lips over her glossy, polished nails. She had been a hand lotion and nail polish addict for years. The final payoff, Nancy thought, half laughing. She glanced nervously around her, but nobody was looking. She considered lifting *his* hands to *her* mouth, but lost her courage. She just didn't know Ben. Imagine being able to make such carefree moves with a strange girl, without a quiver of worry that she'd be irritated, or put him down, or laugh in his face. She herself could never do the same. She'd have to date Ben for months before she reached his stage of confidence.

Date him for months, she thought giddily.

Ben swept the trash off their table and onto the brown plastic trays. Efficiently he dumped the trays into the trash cans and took her arm. Nothing he did was uncertain or insecure.

That's what being a star does to you, Nancy thought. I'm a little bit of a star from cheerleading, but he is *truly* a star.

They left, Ben confirming his star status by telling her about his latest college offer. "Yes," he said casually. "The coaches from State University were at that game where we creamed you guys."

Nancy did not enjoy that remark. They had not been creamed. They had put up a terrific fight and just barely lost. She looked away from Ben, wondering just what loyalty to Tarenton required her to say.

"I'm sorry," Ben said softly. "I wouldn't hurt your feelings for the world. But I can't help it that Donny Parrish just isn't in my league. You wouldn't want me to do a mediocre job at anything, would you?"

"No," she said. Impossible to imagine Ben participating in something mediocre.

"Now where do you live? I'll be getting you early in the morning, so I'd better learn the route now while it's still half light." He tucked her in his front seat like a package for the post office. His presumptuousness did not annoy Nancy. On the contrary, she found that she loved being a possession of Ben Adamson.

The minute this comparison crossed her mind, she knew she had the correct word. She was not Nancy Goldstein for this boy. She was simply his possession. He did not feel nervous because he knew he owned her.

And I don't even care, Nancy thought. What's happening to me? She said, "Where are we going tomorrow morning?"

"My surprise."

This was not said in a teasing voice, but matter of factly, brooking no discussion. In this relationship, Ben would make all decisions. Nancy was supposed to be happy about it. Period. She had a flicker of confusion, maybe even dismay, but it passed when Ben pulled into her driveway and took her in his arms. He wasn't tender or caring. Ben Adamson didn't know what tenderness was, but he expressed a passion that Nancy responded to.

If you counted them up, she had only known him for minutes. Minutes in a darkened hallway. Half an hour over a hamburger. And this kiss was more intense than some she and Alex had shared when they were going together for six months.

I like it, Nancy decided. I like a boy who knows what he's doing and where he's going and doesn't fool around getting there.

Ben smiled at her. Nancy was mesmerized by that smile, her head tilted up to absorb it, her thoughts caught on it. The smile vanished as fast as the sun behind a cloud and Ben kissed her another time. Fiercely. He did not give her any participation in this kiss. It was *his* kiss, but it excited her.

"Early," he said, leaning back. "About six." He turned on the ignition as a form of dismissal.

Six, Nancy thought. That meaning getting up at five to fix her hair and all. What a gruesome thought. "Fine," she said.

"Wear something nice," said Ben, as if she would ever have contemplated wearing something ugly. He leaned across her, opened the door from the inside handle, and waited for her to scoot out. She shut the door herself and he backed out of the driveway without glancing her way again. What a strange combination of business and flirtation he was!

All over Tarenton, people began getting ready for supper.

They were washing hands, peeling potatoes, putting water on to boil, setting tables, calling children in from play, and turning off the television.

Angie Poletti regretfully hung up the phone from talking to her darling Marc, still off at college, and unable to come home again this weekend.

Mary Ellen Kirkwood grated cheese for a macaroni casserole and wept because Donny had not spoken to her after practice.

Olivia Evans stood in her room in front of the

mirror, reliving the heady excitement of the applause she had heard during her most daring leap. Then she went downstairs to have another argument with her mother over whether she ought to be on the squad, or ought to stay home and get a good healthy rest.

Walt Manners did his homework alone over a frozen dinner, while his parents worked late on a tape of their morning show.

And in Mrs. Oetjen's office, Pres Tilford was begging. He had never begged for anything before. Never known the sick taste of being at someone's mercy. Never known the humiliation and agony of having to plead, and of knowing that he might lose.

And all this — in front of Kerry.

"It wasn't me," Pres said, trying to keep his voice from rising with anger and fear. Important to stay calm. If he screamed at Mrs. Oetjen, he would certainly never convince her. And above all, he'd better not throw anything. "I did do it that one time. I admit that. I was —" he took a deep breath. Only the truth could possibly work now: "I was showing off for Kerry. This boy up ahead of us was making shoe marks real high. Kerry was joking that we should catch him and draft him for the cheerleading squad, so we could make use of those unbelievable jumps. And it kind of irritated me that she didn't think *I* could jump like that, so I showed off. And you were there."

Mrs. Oetjen clearly did not believe a word of this.

Kerry said softly, "Please believe us. Really and truly this was the only time and it was my fault. I goaded him into it." Her voice trembled. The thought of the police coming, of Pres being charged with a crime, made her literally ill. She was afraid she was going to throw up, and she knew that Mrs. Oetjen felt nothing but contempt for her, with her trembly little voice and her shaky little hands.

And Pres — what did he feel? Resentment? Rage?

"So what did this other boy look like?" Mrs. Oetjen asked grimly.

Pres and Kerry exchanged hopeless looks. "Well," Pres said slowly, "we couldn't really see him. There was too much sun. He was just sort of a shape up ahead."

"Uh huh," the principal said skeptically. She picked up the telephone and started punching the little square buttons. Pres and Kerry watched with fatalistic silence.

If she calls the police, Pres thought, what am I going to do? My family will kill me. Kerry will dump me. I'll be thrown off the squad. I'll never get into a decent college, either, with a police record.

A record.

It chilled him to the marrow. And for something he hadn't even done! How unfair!

But he knew the number she was ringing, and it wasn't the police. It was Tarenton Fabricators. Pres didn't know but that the police would be preferable to dealing with his father. Preston Tilford II in a towering rage had always managed to terrify Preston Tilford III.

But he doubted if Mrs. Oetjen could get through to his father anyway. Tilford had a viciously protective secretary. She never let anybody talk to Mr. Tilford unless it was previously arranged.

Pres had not reckoned with Mrs. Oetjen's determination. She breezed past that secretary as if she were the President of the United States. "Mr. Tilford?" said Mrs. Oetjen sharply. And she began her version of the story. The high school was covered with black skid marks three, four, and five feet high off the floor. There were even some on the ceiling in the chemistry room, though she didn't know how Pres had done that.

"He didn't," Kerry murmured. "He isn't taking chemistry this year."

Mrs. Oetjen paid no attention to Kerry.

Pres, she informed the boy's father, had been caught in the act, but was nevertheless, in a very sneaky way, trying to get out of it.

Pres Tilford had many faults, but sneakiness was not one of them. More than anything else he hated that accusation. If I *were* doing it, he thought, I'd brag about it. I'd do it out front. I

74

wouldn't sneak around, letting other people take the blame.

His father was so upset he was shouting into the phone. Pres and Kerry could hear his end of the conversation, as if he'd been in the room with them. "I understand the gravity of the situation, Mrs. Oetjen," said Mr. Tilford, "and I certainly thank you for calling me immediately. I am not asking for any special favors for my son, but would you hold off on calling the police until I have a chance to get to the school and talk to Pres myself?"

Pres held his breath.

Mrs. Oetjen agreed.

The three of them sat in her office as the sun set. There was nothing more to say. Pres was afraid if he talked again, he'd start swearing and that would definitely not help his case. Kerry was afraid if she started talking, she'd cry.

The phone rang.

Mrs. Oetjen answered in monosyllables and this time her eyes fixed with acid disgust on Kerry. "Your parents have been out looking for you for the last hour. Do you recall promising them to be home by five, so you could all drive to your aunt's house and go out for dinner?"

Kerry's heart sank. "Now I remember," she whispered.

"They will be here to pick you up at the front door. Kerry, I also thought more highly of *you*! Not only are you aiding and abetting in vandalism, but you are causing your family serious worry that something happened to you. Just so you could be in the company of a boy who clearly isn't worth it."

Kerry Elliot was not a stalwart soul. She took whatever any adult dished out. Shyness and insecurity kept her from ever talking back. But this she could not tolerate. She said without raising her voice, "Mrs. Oetjen, I think you are leaping to conclusions. I thought more highly of *you* also. You are so angry about the defacing of this school, that you're grabbing the first available scapegoat. Well, it isn't Pres doing this. We've both given you our word on that. You ought to know both Pres and me well enough to give us the benefit of the doubt. It hurts me that you won't even listen to us."

Pres was immeasurably touched. A testimony on his behalf. He knew what effort it took such a shy girl to speak like that, knew that she was trembling at the after effect, and took her hand. He squeezed it very lightly. It was cold and damp.

Mrs. Oetjen softened.

For a moment Pres thought they would clear it all up right then. That somehow it would all be okay, and he'd have gotten out of this mess without much problem after all.

But his father stalked into the room.

Mr. Tilford was tall, greying at the temples, wearing glasses that gave his expression an indefinable intensity. He wore a three-piece suit of dark grey, and a quietly patterned tie with a small clip. He looked utterly conservative, law-abiding, and upstanding. He also looked like the sort of man who would not tolerate a son like Pres. He did not so much as look at his son.

He said, "Mrs. Oetjen, I would like to suggest that I take on Pres's punishment myself. I will have him removed from the cheerleading squad. I will take away his Porsche, which we should never have given him in the first place, considering his lack of maturity. And we will ground him, so he won't be in the company of a girl who is such a bad influence."

Pres was on his feet in a shot. "Bad influence!" he shouted. "Kerry is the best influence in my life. How dare you say that about her! Kerry is good. She would never —" He was suddenly aware that he was advancing on his own father. That his fists were doubled and his muscles painfully tensed. It appalled him. Much as they argued in the Tilford household, nobody had ever thought of hitting.

But he was thinking of it now.

Kerry was up and tugging at him. "Pres, no. Don't. Just stay calm." Her soft, vulnerable features came between him and the implacable strength of his father. "He's upset," said Kerry, excusing the terrible remark. "It's natural he'd say things like that right now."

She's right, Pres thought. It is natural for my father to say rotten things.

"All of you please sit down," Mrs. Oetjen said crisply. You, too, Mr. Tilford."

The force of her personality was such that they all obeyed, however reluctantly, lowering themselves slowly into chairs, so that the wooden arms of the chairs kept them safely apart.

"Since my original call to you," Mrs. Oetjen said to Pres's father, "we have done a bit more talking. Kerry has had some sensible and thought-provoking things to say. I have decided to give Pres the benefit of the doubt. I do not see how we are going to test his guilt, or lack of it, because the boy doing this vandalism is very sneaky. If the marking stops, then probably it *is* Pres, unwilling to get caught a second time. If it continues, I still will not know who is doing it." She looked sadly at Pres and Kerry.

I've got to thank her, Pres thought, but he still felt so much like hitting that he did not dare utter a syllable or make a move.

Kerry said, "Thank you, Mrs. Oetjen." She thought, Terrific. Now Pres and I are going to have to catch this person who's really doing it, or be under suspicion for the rest of the school year.

"Nevertheless," Mr. Tilford said, "you are grounded, Pres. No dates. No cheerleading."

He had known it was coming. And he had known just how powerless he was to do anything about it. He could not cheerlead on the sly, because Ardith would be informed and have auditions to replace him. He could not date Kerry on the sly, because his father would call her parents and that would end that.

His rage grew.

Talk about a soap opera, Pres thought. Calm down, Pres old boy. Calm down.

Kerry's cool fingers rested on his taut muscles. Lightly, ever so lightly, she massaged them, saying the same thing with her touch, but more effectively, more lovingly: *Stay calm.*

Mrs. Oetjen said, "I believe that if we give the benefit of the doubt in one way, we should do it in all ways, Mr. Tilford. I would be against denying them each other's company and equally against taking Pres off the squad. If they are given a chance, it must be a whole chance, not a fractional chance."

She was like a block of granite. Kerry was filled with admiration for her obstinance. She could not know that Mr. Tilford looked at this woman with even more admiration.

Like to have her working for Tarenton Fabricators, he thought. She's wasted at a school. She should be in manufacturing, a strong woman like that. He accepted her decision. "Pres," he said to his son, "you are a very fortunate boy."

The office door slammed open and Kerry's mother and father burst into the room.

"Oh, no," Kerry cried. "I forgot *again*. I was supposed to meet you outside. Mom, I'm really sorry." She stood up fast, and Pres stood up right beside her, so they were a team giving each other support.

"Kerry," her mother said, tense and exasperated, "I am seriously thinking of grounding you."

Mrs. Oetjen laughed, Mr. Tilford laughed, and the surprise of their laughter was so great that Pres and Kerry giggled, too. "We just dismissed that as a possibility," Mrs. Oetjen said, smiling at the Elliots and giving them a fuller explanation. "Let's let these two sort out their own problems. As for the vandalism, I'll have to find another way to deal with it."

She turned to Pres, with a heaviness in her manner that chilled him a second time. "If you *are* doing this, Preston," she said quietly, "it will be the police we call and not your family. I will bring criminal charges against you. Do you understand?"

CHAPTER

Mary Ellen wept over Donny until quarter to eight. She stopped not because of homework that had to be done, but because the sobbing was giving her a terrible headache.

How could there be such perfection in life one day, and such misery the next?

How *could* Ben have done such a thing?

Mary Ellen raged at Ben . . . and at Donny.

Who was Donny, to let Ben take control like that? Patrick stood up to Ben. Patrick kept Tarenton's honor. Donny just sat there, taking it. Letting Ben own the Tarenton gym.

Don't think about Patrick, she told herself. Forget about Patrick. If you *can*, a small voice said.

At quarter to eight, Mary Ellen pressed a cold, wet washcloth to her forehead and began her English homework. Shakespeare. Mary Ellen had not told anybody, but she truly loved Shakespeare. She loved to whisper the lines, hearing their symmetry and their style. This was the fourth play they'd studied in high school: *Macbeth.*

Such tough, determined people. The characters in *Macbeth* knew what they wanted, and they went out and got it.

Amoral, maybe. But achievers. Mary Ellen respected achievers.

Would I rather be one of the witches, she thought, or Lady Macbeth?

Right now she felt witchy. She felt like bending over a great bubbling cauldron, coming up with vicious spells and cruel concoctions. She saw herself: dark and dank and stringy and mean. Casting a spell on Nancy, who had brought Ben into their lives and taken the glow off Donny.

The phone rang.

I come, Greymalkin, Mary Ellen thought. *Fair is foul and foul is fair.* "Hello," she said sweetly.

"Hello." It was a heavy, masculine voice. She knew the speaker, but she couldn't quite place him. After a moment of confusion, she said, "How are you?" which seemed safe.

"Okay."

Two syllables. No clues. But if the call had been for Gemma or her parents, the voice would have said so. It was her call. "I'm doing my Shakespeare," she said.

"What a horrible thought."

Donny. Was it Donny? She could not tell. She had talked to Donny only once on the telephone. Stupid as it seemed, she could not absolutely recognize his voice. Once, months ago, Mary Ellen had publicly mistaken Patrick for Pres, making a total fool of herself. She would not address this boy by name until she was one hundred percent sure.

"I love Shakespeare," he confided.

"You're kidding."

"What can I say? I like older men."

A shout of laughter.

So it was Donny, definitely Donny. His laughter was most unusual, a true shout. Literally gales of laughter. She loved Donny's laugh. How wonderful to hear it now, and know that she had brought it to him! That he'd called in spite of the afternoon's fiasco. She would willingly have hugged a porcupine, she was so pleased. The world that had rated dark tears became a world of sunshine.

"I hate Shakespeare," Donny said. In emphatic detail, he told Mary Ellen what he held against Shakespeare. Poor Shakespeare, thought Mary Ellen.

She held the phone with her left hand, scribbled her analysis with her right, and chatted happily with Donny for an hour.

Gemma, her younger sister, sat in the kitchen. She had heard the phone ring, heard the delighted peal of laughter, knew that there was an admiring boy on the phone.

Cheerleading was supposed to make Mary Ellen's life terrific, Gemma mused. I guess it does, sometimes. But sometimes it seems to me that the closer Mary Ellen gets to Number One, the harder she has to struggle to stay there.

Much as she idolized her sister, Gemma wondered if she would want to be on Varsity when she was old enough to try out.

But Mary Ellen Kirkwood had no such qualms. She had a great capacity to enjoy the moment — and this moment was *hers*.

Very early the following morning, Ben Adamson pulled into the Goldstein driveway and tapped lightly on the horn. He made no move to come to the door. Nancy waved through the window that she had seen him and was coming. As she gathered her books, Mrs. Goldstein remarked, "Always be careful of a boy who expects *you* to go to *him*."

"It wouldn't be efficient for him to stop the engine and walk up to the door when I'm on my way out," Nancy said.

"Boyfriends shouldn't worry about efficiency," her mother said.

Nancy chose not to pay attention. She zipped her heavy jacket and took a final glance in the mirror. The scarlet of her jacket set off her dark, thick hair beautifully. She looked just the way she wanted to look. Lovely.

They were going somewhere for breakfast, she would have a wonderful time, and Ben would have something grand planned for Saturday night. The fact that in one short week there'd be a tough, angry grudge match against Garrison, with her cheering Donny and not Ben, was something Nancy could not deal with right now.

Her mother said softly, "Nanny, honey, I'm not sure about this arrangement."

Her mother had not called her Nanny in ages. Nancy said, "Mother, really. Everything's fine. I can handle it."

"I'm not so sure," Mrs. Goldstein said, but she did nothing to interfere. Nancy left quickly and got into the car with Ben.

He literally filled the front seat. She had never felt so dwarfed, or so happy, or so tense. She wanted to snuggle up against him, but he made no move toward her. He just drove. She sat on her side, feeling like a mouse next to him. She could not take her eyes off him.

It was not that he was good looking. It was that he had so much personality, you were forced to look at him.

"Where are we going?" Nancy asked.

She generally had some breakfast at school. The junior class sold donuts, Danish, coffee, and orange juice, and kept the profits for their dances and activities, and it was infinitely more fun to breakfast there (on her pitiful glass of orange juice) in good company than to bother with it at home. She knew she'd never run into any high school kids this morning because if they had breakfast out, they'd have it at school.

A breakfast date, she thought. Not very romantic.

It was very cold, but Ben wasn't wearing much. A sleeveless ski vest over a wool plaid shirt. On another boy, thinner and less impressive, this would have been an attempt to be macho. But Ben was the living definition of macho. On him it was real. Compared to Ben, all boys Nancy had ever known seemed wimpy.

Ben turned north and headed into the deep woods. Nancy was startled. There weren't any towns out this way. There wasn't much of anything out this way except trees, forests, lakes, and narrow logging roads.

Ben said, "I'm going to be on television."

Nancy gasped. "You *are*! Tell me about it!"

"You know the Manners' show?"

Of course she did. Aside from the fact that Walt's parents *were* "Breakfast at Home," she'd watched it nearly every weekday morning since moving to Tarenton. She loved the whole format, and so did her mother and father.

"Well," Ben said, "they're doing a segment on sought-after high school athletes. College scholar-

86

ships. That kind of thing." Thick pride was in his voice.

She wondered how she was going to see this through. How she was going to face Walt, when she was with Ben. How did this happen to me? she cried silently.

Nancy said thickly, "That's exciting. I guess there was nobody to interview but you, Ben."

Immediately she felt like a genuine traitor. There was Donny Parrish. He was pretty darn sought after. Flushing slightly, imagining her Varsity Squad listening to this conversation, Nancy stared out the window. Trees. Endless trees of the North Woods. The road seemed vaguely familiar, though.

"Tell me about your offers," she said.

"You aren't a spy for Tarenton, are you?" he asked teasingly.

Nancy protested, "Ben, I am one hundred percent on your team." The words did not gag her. They came out easily. They shocked her, though. How can I, Nancy Goldstein, Tarenton Varsity cheerleader, tell this boy I'm one hundred percent for the opposite team? she wondered.

Ben grinned inwardly. He had made a conquest here, that was for sure. How far would this Nancy go to prove she liked him? Well, he would find out Saturday night. He would arrange things so that if she proved the least bit willing, they could go all the way.

* * *

Three years ago, Walt Manners' mother, sick and tired of the same old wallpaper in the family room, stripped it off. It was a laborious task that took her long hours over several sweaty days. Eventually she was down to the plaster of the old walls in the log cabin area of the house. They did not film there, but guests, awaiting their turns, relaxed in this room, adjacent to the kitchen.

What with one thing and another, Mrs. Manners never got around to repapering. Since they expected to cover the wall shortly, they began writing their telephone messages, grocery lists, and family reminders right on the plaster because it was such a large and useful white space next to the phone. Before long, a famous guest happened to jot a message from a still more famous person right there on the wall. Another important guest, impressed by such names, added a little graffiti of his own. Still another drew doodles that had a certain grace and appeal, and these were later included in a huge, penciled cartoon by a famous cartoonist.

The wall became one of the household's most beloved possessions. If you did not like something, you could erase it. Meanwhile, the graffiti collection grew, spreading across the family room and pushing toward the kitchen.

Guests on the "Breakfast at Home" show made references to the wall when they were on the air, and locally it became quite famous. People were always flattered to be asked to sign the wall. The wall was often referred to in conversation. ("I wrote my name over next to the governor's, of course.")

Until the morning that Ben Adamson was the guest on his parents' television show, Walt had no feelings whatsoever about the wall.

He had not known about Ben.

Frequently he had no idea what was going on in the show. When school was demanding, when basketball was in season, when the winter sports he loved were being played, Walt barely noticed his parents. Mr. and Mrs. Manners rose very early in the morning to prepare for the taping. Walt rarely saw them in the morning.

He didn't even tend to watch when he had breakfast. He chose to have his English muffin in peace in the kitchen, away from the action. If he had the kitchen TV on at all, it was usually tuned to cartoons, which he loved.

He paid no attention to his mother's aide, who was setting out freshly perked coffee, juice, and donuts for this morning's guest. He took a donut, wishing it could be chocolate. But they never set out anything sticky. You didn't want a guest with chocolate or cinnamon sugar on his face.

He ate the first donut standing up, staring vaguely out the kitchen window, watching a light snow fall. His parents would be delighted about the snow. The viewers would see it through the great glass windows that faced the woods, and it would lend a real down-home backdrop to the interview.

"Hi, Walt," said a familiar soft voice.

Mouth full of English muffin, jam on his fingers, Walt turned to see Nancy Goldstein looking at him.

He was used to strangers dropping in, but he was not used to friends. The house was much too far off the beaten track for kids to drop in. He felt very self-conscious sucking the jam off his fingers while Nancy stared at him. He felt weird, standing in his kitchen with her there — no explanation, just there.

"I'm here with Ben," she said nervously. "He's going to be interviewed by your parents. He and his coach. He's gotten all those terrific college athletic offers, you know, and there are so many places trying to sign Ben up, so your mother and father are interviewing him."

Nancy looked at Walt, pleadingly. "Look, I didn't know we were coming here. He didn't tell me, until we were on the way. I couldn't. . . ."

Walt couldn't believe it.

Bad enough that his parents were interviewing the star of some other high school, but that Nancy — his co-cheerleader, Nancy — should have come along was like treason. His parents he had to forgive: The show covered a dozen area towns, of which Tarenton was the smallest, and Garrison, in fact, the most important.

But Tarenton was — *had* to be — the most important for Nancy and Walt.

Nancy reached a hand out to touch Walt's arm, asking to be forgiven.

Walt turned away from her and forcefully shoved down the knob on the toaster for his second English muffin.

Ben Adamson entered the kitchen. He had to stoop to come in, the low threshold an obstacle. Stooping made Ben appear even larger, formidable, unbeatable. There were no air spaces around Ben, no glimpse of the room beyond. There was just Ben, and Ben's shoulders. And Ben's condescending smile.

Walt, who was not small, felt small.

If he had felt awkward and irritable with Nancy, he felt deeply trespassed upon by Ben. Guests were not invited into the kitchen. They were supposed to stop at the door, where the aide handed them a donut and a Styrofoam cup of coffee.

Ben sauntered on in, keeping his head low, as if even in the kitchen he would not fit, he being a superstar who needed extra space.

Never had it been so hard for Walt to keep from shouting. As calmly as he could, he said, "Guests normally wait in the other room, Ben."

Ben looked gratified. "You know who I am?" he said. "From basketball, I take it?"

Walt managed not to tell Ben where to take it. He chewed hard on his muffin instead. Nancy stood there, tears gathering in her eyes.

Ben extended a hand to shake.

What timing, Walt thought. I've got butter and jam on my hands. Then he thought, What better person to get a little stickiness and grease on? He shook hands eagerly, and smiled to himself as Ben realized he now had a very messy hand and nothing to wipe it on.

Won that round, Walt thought with satisfaction.

"Walt's a cheerleader with me," Nancy said, trying to ease the tension.

Ben laughed. Actually *laughed*. Clearly the thought of a boy cheerleader was comical to Ben.

I will not hit him, Walt thought.

Ben began reading the wall graffiti out loud. Naturally he picked the supremely stupid ones. "Call plumber to take out toilet before linoleum goes down," Ben said, laughing again. "You people immortalize all the really important things, don't you?"

I could dismember him, Walt thought. But Mom wouldn't like blood all over the floor.

Ben's bleak face held its contained but deep amusement. Amusement at Walt's expense. Then Ben laughed *again*, that ragged, rough laugh that made Walt feel furious and made Nancy giggle in panic. "I can't believe what you're watching on this television," Ben said.

"What's he watching?" Nancy asked.

"Mighty Mouse cartoons." Ben doubled over with laughter. Ben doubled over took up all the free space in the entire kitchen.

Walt did not know what he might have done if his mother hadn't appeared in the doorway. She was wearing a soft wool dress, smelling of lilac perfume and looked pretty, warm, and welcoming. "So this is Ben Adamson," she said in her throaty voice. "I've heard *so* much about you." She extended a hand and did not flinch or comment on the jam and butter that were now passed to her. She was far too poised. She explained just how the filming would go: where Ben would sit, where his coach would sit, the sort of questions they would be asked, where to direct their gazes during the interview. Ben listened intently. There would be no flubs in his first TV appearance. Ben was not the type to get flustered under pressure. He thrived on it.

Probably get offered a job as an anchor as well as a full scholarship to college, Walt thought morosely. He thought if Nancy said one more word of explanation, he would shove her into the toaster.

Mrs. Manners took Ben into the living room, shutting the thick kitchen door tightly behind her. Quickly Walt changed TV stations so they'd be tuned to the Manners' show.

"You can watch Mighty Mouse," Nancy said.

Walt's mother came into focus. The camera turned to Ben. "I *am* watching Mighty Mouse," Walt said.

"Oh, Walt, if I'd known. . . ."

"I think it's the perfect name." Walt said, ignoring Nancy. He hoped Ben would be awful. His mother would say, "And were you surprised to win by such a wide margin?" and Ben would say, "Unhhh, dduuhhh, welll, guess not, uhhhh."

But no such luck. Mighty Mouse chatted away like somebody up for a professorship. Then his mother did it to him. She said, smiling sweetly, "And what are your biggest plans for the moment, Ben?"

A sharp smile decorated the hawklike face. "Whipping Tarenton. But it won't be hard. They don't have much to offer."

CHAPTER

It wasn't so much that the Tarenton High students were rude to Nancy. In the short time she'd lived in Tarenton, she had proved herself a good kid and a good friend. They just didn't bother with her at all. She wasn't included in the chatter and she wasn't in on the jokes. She was just there on the sidelines, watching.

It was like being new in school all over again. Unnoticed. Unwanted.

Except for Vanessa Barlow. Vanessa never let a chance to attack Nancy go by. She did it blatantly, not trying to be clever. She simply let Nancy know, in every way she could, that she thought Nancy was a traitor.

Walt managed to get out of any blame for his

parents' interview by referring to Ben Adamson as Mighty Mouse. Tarenton loved it. The nickname was picked up instantly. "Did you hear what Mighty Mouse said?" went the talk up and down the halls. "Mighty Mouse doesn't think we have anything to offer."

Mary Ellen said firmly to Donny, "We'll show Mighty Mouse, won't we?"

Olivia said to Mary Ellen, "Wait till Mighty Mouse sees the new routine we've got. We can cream Garrison any *place*, any *time*."

Nobody said anything to Nancy Goldstein.

She did not know what to do about her divided feelings. Of course she didn't want Tarenton beaten! But neither did she want Ben beaten, not when he was on this fabulous winning streak. And, maybe, herself beside him.

During English, she paid no attention to the lecture on Shakespeare. She made a mental ledger and weighed having Ben against not having Ben. As long as her name was linked with his, even a little bit, she had no friends, no companionship, no shared laughter. But she did have the hope of being Ben's girl, and never, *never*, had she met a more exciting boy.

It was not a good day for her.

But like all days, it ended eventually. She went to cheerleading practice, grateful to be with the only group that had any use for her.

But today was different.

Today she was the traitor in their midst, and

they resented having to use her at all. When Nancy spoke, they said, "Listen, Goldstein, we'll do it our way. Play games with Mighty Mouse if you don't like it."

When Nancy got tired, they said, "What's your problem? You trying to sabotage our practice? Throw the ball to Mighty Mouse, maybe? Keep working, Nancy."

I can't do it, Nancy thought. I'm not strong enough. I can't stand up to them.

But then she remembered Ben, who could stand up to anybody, and it gave her strength. She shrugged off their attitudes and kept working on Tarenton cheers, thinking of a Garrison boy.

Mrs. Evans rumbled into the gym on Thursday afternoon. They had been practicing for a hour and they were tired, sweaty, disheveled, and snapping at each other. Carrying her own chair, she marched in, thrust the folding metal chair with its padded seat into the floor as if it were a stake at which someone would burn, and said harshly, "Olivia? What are you doing? That looks very dangerous to me."

"Oh, no, Mother," said Olivia. "It's quite ordinary."

Nobody met anybody else's eyes. Mrs. Evans was totally right. It was a dangerous routine. "In fact, I think we'll do it again," Olivia said brightly. She turned to the squad, her whole posture one of daring, of *I'll show my mother a thing or two.* In rhythm, she yelled, "Are you *ready*?"

They rose to the occasion. "We're *ready*."

"Roadway, runway, *rail*way,". Olivia led the cheer. They began their new motions.

"Make this game our vict'ry day!"

Olivia pirouetted dramatically back beyond the rest of the squad. In perfect symmetry, their arms at precisely the same height, their legs lifted in kicks, their feet smacking the gym floor for noisy emphasis, the other five took new positions. "*Allllll the way!*" they screamed. "*Allllll the way!*"

Olivia ran. Hurtling through the air, she leaped, her right foot touching Pres's cupped palms lightly. He thrust up, and this time Olivia flipped over the outstretched fingertips of the girls, landing by a crouching Walt, and flipped over him, to end in a somersault, then a split. The girls moved forward flashing their scarlet and white pompons like a bouquet of flowers, and Walt and Pres leaped up on the sides and came down in matching poses opposite Olivia.

Wow, Pres thought. He didn't suppose he'd ever get used to that cheer. It scared him that he might foul up and it would end with Olivia getting hurt.

He wished his parents would come to the game Friday against Grove Hill. Grove Hill wasn't much of a team and it would be an easy win, as long as Tarenton didn't get cocky. But it was a time to practice their spectacular routines, the ones that would help in the downfall of Mighty Mouse.

But his mother had gone to Scotland for ten days and was due back tonight. She would still be too tired to attend a school basketball game. Actually, the Tilfords were too tired to attend any game where their son humiliated them by cheering, but Pres chose not to think of that at this moment. He just hoped she'd come back from Scotland in a better mood than she'd left.

"I won't have it!" Mrs. Evans screamed. "Won't have what?" Ardith said innocently.

"Won't have my little girl risking her life like this!"

"I'm not risking my life, Mother. I'm just showing off the skills *you* gave me, Mother, when you paid for those gymnastics and fencing lessons all these years."

"This is not what I had in mind!" Mrs. Evans said.

"But it *is* what I have in mind," Olivia answered.

They were stalemated. Mrs. Evans, woman of steel, had inadvertently raised a daughter of steel.

Ardith said meekly, "I wouldn't allow Olivia to do this if I really thought she could hurt herself, Mrs. Evans."

"Then you aren't really watching," Olivia's mother said. "I cannot believe you are encouraging this sort of maneuver. Whatever happened to the nice cheers? The sweet friendly ones, like 'Go Get 'em'?"

"Go Get 'em" was the least sweet cheer imaginable, with a final line describing the blood and guts that would spill before the game was out, but nobody felt like arguing with Mrs. Evans. Ardith walked her toward the door. Olivia muttered, "Let's get out of here while the getting's good."

"You can't leave," Angie objected. "Your mother will kill you."

"I'm going," Olivia said. "Who volunteers to give me a ride home?"

"None of us wants to tangle with your mother," Pres said. "Especially me. I've got my own mother to cope with tonight."

"I thought your mother was away," Mary Ellen said.

"Yes, but she's coming back." Pres made it sound like the second eruption of a volcano.

Mary Ellen was in a very expansive mood. The world was going her way again. Ben had been reduced effectively to a cartoon mouse; Donny had called her, sat with her at lunch; Nancy was nothing but a trespasser instead of a threat; and the squad had done so wonderfully during practice that *nobody* could ever call them second best again. She said, "Olivia, I'll ride home with you so that your mother can yell at me instead of you."

"Mary Ellen," Olivia said, "you are a true saint."

"Well, for a minute or two anyway," Mary Ellen said honestly, laughing.

"You aren't riding home with Olivia," Donny Parrish said, appearing from nowhere, grinning down at them all. "Olivia's riding with us. I'll drop her off on our way to get a bite to eat before I take you home."

All eyes inspected Donny. It was partly for him they were going through such effort. If Donny were less of a player, or less of a person, they would surrender to the inevitable and let Ben Adamson and Garrison take the championship.

Donny satisfied them.

Tall, rangy, broad, and competent, he looked the way a good basketball player ought to look. A nice, wholesome grin decorated a nice — Mary Ellen caught the word *bland* going through her mind and killed it — face. *Handsome*, she told herself. Future ahead. Going places.

Mary Ellen and Olivia went off on either side of Donny, and he escorted them as if it were his honor.

Standing behind, Pres murmured to Walt, "The trouble is that Ben will be showing off for our Nancy. Ben's going to try harder just because of Nancy."

"Nancy is welcome to move back to Ohio this afternoon," Walt said.

"Women are nothing but trouble," Pres said, thinking of Nancy and his mother.

Kerry walked into the gym and Pres said, "But there are exceptions."

He and Walt laughed.

The afternoon with Kerry put Pres in a wonderful frame of mind. He even thought of it as an entire afternoon with her, although it had been less than three quarters of an hour, really. The practice dwindled in his mind and the moments with Kerry expanded, and his thoughts dwelled on the kisses they had shared and the closeness of their thoughts instead of the strife at school.

Because of Kerry he met his mother at the airport cheerfully, and gave her a genuine kiss and listened to her chatter about Scotland.

That night, after a late dinner, the three Tilfords were sitting in the most elegant room in the huge old Victorian mansion. Furnished with his great-grandmother's belongings, it was red velvet, ornate walnut, and scrolled chair legs. By the firelight his mother sparkled.

She began handing out the presents she had brought them. She had actually brought a kilt for his father. Pres tried to imagine his father in a kilt and failed.

"I hope you've brought a kilt for our son, too," Mr. Tilford said. His voice was cutting, but Felicia was too happy to hear it. Pres picked it up immediately and waited for the sniping to begin.

"So what did you bring me, Mom?" Pres asked.

"It's something for you to wear," she said. "And I want you to promise me you'll wear it to school tomorrow."

"If it's a kilt," said Pres, "I will never even unpack it."

"It's not a kilt," she promised, and she handed him a large package.

CHAPTER

Kerry Elliot's life was built upon tiny glimpses of Pres. She cherished every conversation they ever had. At night, lying snuggled under layers of quilts, she would run through the conversations again until she had them by memory, like so many hit songs.

In school, having memorized his schedule and his habits, she had found ways to see him in the distance. She had told nobody — not even Pres — that she was doing this. It was her private joy, to spot Pres when he was unaware of her. To know that this fabulous boy was hers, that that wonderful young man sauntering around the corner would drive her home in his red Porsche that very day.

Each day she ran the long way between biology and English, because if she was lucky, she'd see Pres and Troy and Donny together, going from their gym class to Spanish.

The three walked in that space-taking manner important boys had, and the momentary glimpse of Pres's dark-blond head laughing next to Donny's kept Kerry buoyed with happiness for the next two classes, before she sat with him at lunch.

Today Kerry felt wonderful.

She was no longer worried about the vandalism. It was still going on. In fact, there were new shoe marks in the foyer that very morning.

And the sweater was almost done. Kerry was so excited by being so close to the finished product. All those hours! Every stitch a stitch for Pres.

Kerry decided not to wait for Pres's birthday. Too far off.

Besides, the weather was cold right now. He *needed* her sweater. She'd give it to him hot off the needles, so to speak. Maybe Saturday night? At the celebration when they whipped Garrison? (Or the funeral if Garrison whipped them.)

Kerry rushed from biology to get to the west wing in time to spot the boys. She arrived just as Donny appeared, a head taller than the others, but not, to Kerry's eyes, nearly as appealing. Too ordinary, which was an odd thing to think of a star like Donny Parrish. And yet, that's what

Donny was. Bland. Troy followed Donny, and then Kerry saw —

Her sweater.

Her wool.

Her design.

On Pres.

Kerry felt as if she had been hit by a truck.

Hours . . . hours . . . *hours* of love, and the offering was ruined.

Pres had not gone to her house, sneaked into her bedroom, gotten the all-but-one-inch finished sweater out of its tote bag, finished the neckband himself, and worn it to surprise her. Somebody else had given it to him.

It could only be his mother. His mother who arrived back from Scotland last night. Scotland, where you could buy wonderful handknits.

Tears rose in Kerry's eyes. No, the pattern wasn't identical, but the style and weight of the yarn was. How much thrill would there be in her gift now? She could not speak. A hot, thick lump blocked her throat. Don't see me, Pres, she prayed. It was the reverse of her usual prayer: *See me, Pres*, see me.

She was going to cry. She knew it. Kerry loathed crying. It took her like a virus: an implacable, destructive illness that, once it took hold, could wipe her away. Once her tear ducts opened, they stayed open for days.

I cannot give in, she thought. If so much as

one tear overflows, I will weep all day, through every class.

"Kerry?" said a friend of hers. "Did you get that math problem on the second page?"

Kerry could not even focus on the friend to identify her. She nodded blindly. Math rarely troubled her.

"I didn't understand a single problem," another girl said glumly. "I hate math. Why do we have to study it anyhow? We can use calculators whenever we need to know something."

"It's good for us," the first girl said. "Builds our characters."

This is good for me, Kerry told herself. It's going to build my character. Isn't that wonderful? Isn't it great to know how strong I'm going to be, because I had my heart set on giving Pres the sweater of his life? Isn't it terrific to know that I, Kerry Elliot, spent dozens and dozens of hours for no purpose except to strengthen my character?

Kerry willed her tears away.

It was a sweater, nothing more. A little wool, a little time killed. She could give it to Pres anyhow. At least he'd know she made the effort. Or she could give it to her father or brother, who both yearned for it.

Or she could lie down here on the math room floor, wailing and gnashing her teeth and beating her fists. Kerry estimated how many calories she would use up having the temper tantrum of the century. Enough to lose the weight she would like to take off? There should be a silver lining in every cloud; maybe this would be the silver lining.

Five minutes before the bell rang, just as she was congratulating herself on self-control, the kind she deserved a gold medal for, the teacher announced a surprise quiz.

The class looked at him in disgust. Quizzes were rotten enough, but surprise quizzes?

Like doom, the teacher passed out mimeographed sheets — half sheets actually — with six problems. When there were so few problems, you knew they would all be terrible. On the other hand, there were only five minutes left in the class. How terrible could they be with so little time to work them out?

Kerry lifted her pencil and that tiny act brought memory flooding over her. A day one month ago . . . sitting in Pres's kitchen . . . Pres running upstairs to get something for his mother. . . . Mrs. Tilford, who was no fan of Kerry's, asking why Kerry was leafing through a book of sweater patterns . . . Kerry flipping to the page where she was using a pencil stub for a marker and showing her the sweater she was knitting for Pres . . . Mrs. Tilford saying nothing good or bad about the idea . . . Kerry swiftly shutting the book and saying nothing herself because Pres was thundering down the stairs again and whirling into the kitchen.

She did it on purpose, Kerry thought.

Pres's mother did that on purpose! She went out and bought a sweater just like the one I was knitting for him. She wouldn't let some dull little chubby sophomore give her precious son something special.

Kerry's pencil moved independently, solving the problems on the math quiz, checking answers, doing proofs.

Kerry's eyes saw Felicia Tilford. Beautiful, oh so beautiful. But shallow. And perhaps not very nice. Whenever Pres said bad things about his parents, Kerry always stood up for them. Maybe she was wrong. Maybe they didn't deserve her support.

Maybe Felicia Tilford was truly capable of treachery.

Kerry shook herself and the pencil made a long, black, stabbing line across the half page. Treachery was much too strong a word. It was just a sweater, after all.

She had gotten into the habit of exaggerating because of the anger over Garrison, over Ben Adamson, over Nancy Goldstein. They were calling all three The Enemy now. Poor Nancy.

You couldn't help who you fell in love with.

I suppose, Kerry thought, passing in her paper without noticing, I can't help it that I love Pres, and Mrs. Tilford can't help it that she doesn't like me.

So now what do I do? she thought, changing

classes, calling hello to her friends, waving at the people she knew, smiling at those she didn't. Did she tell Pres what his mother had done? Would he believe her? Did she want Pres to know a bad thing about his mother? Would he think Kerry was crazy to get all worked up over some dumb sweater?

Maybe it would be best for Pres to wear his mother's sweater happily, glad that this gift was not flashlight batteries and socks, proud that she had bothered to think of him when she was abroad.

Why, after all, should Pres know that mixed up in his gift was anger and resentment toward Kerry, and toward them both as a couple?

In the front foyer a tall, slim, dark boy, wearing cheap shoes with heavy black rubbery soles, walked silently. Sun splashed across the foyer with a glaring intensity. Clear on the foyer walls were wide streaks of fresh white paint, blotches covering the shoe marks of the week before.

He was not a bad person. He would not hit somebody, or steal, or peddle drugs, or even say vicious things. He had never done anything against school rules. In fact, he had never done anything at all.

He had little personality and fewer skills. Never gotten a high mark. Never made a team. Never been told a paper was excellent. Never had his artwork hung on the wall.

And suddenly, all he had to do was run down a hall, leap into the air while still running, leave a footprint, and the entire school was talking about him. Principals were after his skin. Kids admired his anonymous ability to jump high. And now, indelibly, his artwork was on the walls.

He liked sneaking. Nobody knew. Nobody suspected. He liked that. It was a secret to hug to himself: dark and wrong and successful.

To think that Mrs. Oetjen suspected Pres Tilford. It was comical really. Pres, of wealth and good looks, sophistication and beautiful girls. Pres, who could get away with anything because of who he was. Preston Tilford III. In deep and serious trouble.

An extra dose of vandalism. First the walls. Then Pres. He had vandalized Pres. Pulled him in, pulled him down, and Pres had no choice. Pres, who could make any choice, had no choice at all.

The boy thought, I'll leave the walls alone until after cheerleading practice. Nobody notices me. They won't remember I've been hanging around. The moment Varsity leaves the gym, but before Pres can go out to that Porsche of his, I'll do it.

He would never own a Porsche.

But he could get Pres in enough trouble that Pres would lose the Porsche.

Heady thought, all that power. The boy laughed to himself, and put a hand over his mouth to hide the amusement, lest somebody suspect, and think, and draw conclusions.

TGIF, Nancy Goldstein said, eight hundred times.

She even made it into a cheer inside her head. Thank God it's Friday. Yea, rah-rah, *Friday*!

School, which she normally loved, would be over. In the brief time she'd known Ben, school had become a silent torture.

Tonight she would go out with Ben. And Saturday, too.

The weekend seemed complex beyond all imagining. Nancy couldn't see how she was going to cope.

The game against Grove Hill would be their first time showing off the brilliant, daring cheers that made her so anxious. And post-game celebrations would not exactly be a source of relaxation either.

She had agreed to meet Ben at the Tarenton Burger House after the game. He would be coming from (presumably) *his* basketball victory game in Garrison, and she would be coming from (she hoped) *her* victory. And then what? Would they sit there, just the two of them, pretending they hadn't noticed that they were on opposite teams?

She could hardly invite him to Pres's party. He'd be killed.

There were unexpected advantages to having

Pres date Kerry. It had made Pres a host. Nancy wasn't sure why. Perhaps Pres had not wanted sharp, hard Vanessa or glossy, demanding Mary Ellen on his home territory, but once he had Kerry at his side, he could welcome the world.

And it pretty much *would* be their world. The basketball team and their dates, the Varsity Squad and their dates, plus assorted friends nobody could party without. Nancy could not bear missing it. Parties like that were half the reason she tried out for cheerleading to start with. But to bring Ben was unthinkable. And meeting a boy like Ben was the other half of her reason for being a cheerleader, and she wasn't about to give him up either.

But Friday night was a mere nothing compared to Saturday.

Nancy's head ached whenever she contemplated Saturday. Ben would play against Donny. She would cheer for Donny. She would participate in those terrifying leaps and precisely timed moves for Donny's sake, while Ben — tall, rugged Ben — would be right there. And everyone on the Tarenton side of the gym would watch her to see how she handled it.

Maybe I'll just get sick, Nancy thought.

Back in Ohio, Nancy had found getting sick to be an excellent way of removing herself from unpleasant situations. But it wouldn't work now. She was too old. A ten-year-old could play games like that, but Nancy couldn't. Furthermore, she was a squad member, and she had no right to damage Varsity just because of her discomfort.

And what would happen after the game?

If Tarenton lost (it was beyond bearing — they *had* to win!) would she really have the guts to go out with Ben Adamson and celebrate a Garrison win?

And if Tarenton won (they'd better!) would Ben still be willing to cart her along to whatever miserable excuse for a party his bitterly disappointed team would have? Or not have?

Nancy pressed her hands to a throbbing forehead. How could this have happened to her? Why couldn't you just fall peacefully in love with somebody suitable and go your own private way, making your own private decisions?

School had never seemed like such an imposition. Who could be expected to pay attention to dull things like history and math when they were faced with the kind of decisions Nancy Goldstein had to make this afternoon?

At lunch, Kerry would have preferred not to see Pres. She had the tears under control — but barely. Once she got close to that sweater (and she saw, she was sure, the perfection of its workmanship, the beauty of its pattern, whereas her efforts were just that — efforts), she would crack up.

Kerry would have skipped lunch if her girl friends hadn't linked arms with her and all, unknowingly, dragged her downstairs to the cafeteria. They loved Kerry dating Pres as much as Kerry did. They all hoped they, too, would be noticed by these shining senior boys and asked out. Be able to live in a dream, like Kerry.

Little did they know that the dream could get pretty frayed around the edges.

All cafeteria talk was of basketball games.

"Grove Hill tonight."

"No prob. We'll whip them like cream."

"I'm not even going. I'm saving my throat for Saturday."

"It's going to take more than your screams to knock Ben Adamson out of the game."

"Did you hear that Nancy Goldstein is going out with him?"

"Nancy Goldstein? *Our* Nancy Goldstein?"

"Yes. Isn't that disgusting?"

"And she calls herself a cheerleader. Honestly. If that's the kind of girl they put on Varsity, who needs it?"

"I just hope we don't have to be ashamed of the squad again this week. It was pitiful the way those Garrison cheerleaders showed us up."

Across the cafeteria, Donny and Troy waved at her. Pres wasn't there yet, but they had saved her a place. On other days, Kerry was thrilled with it all — catching signals from boys like that! Today she sagged. Reluctantly she left the safety of her friends and sat with Donny and Troy. Mary Ellen breezed in, looking her goldengirl self. Kerry felt chunky and worthless. Tears attacked the back of her eyes.

Pres walked in. Broad shouldered and oh, so handsome in his new sweater. The first thing he said was, "Like my new sweater, Ker?" He kissed her, which had a ripple effect, because Donny then kissed Mary Ellen and Troy kissed the senior girl who was with him. Kerry didn't even know her.

"My mom brought it from Scotland," Pres said happily. "I was afraid she would bring me a kilt, but she brought me this. Isn't it great? I always wanted a handknit sweater like this."

So that's what it means to rub salt in the open wound, Kerry thought, wincing. She smiled at Pres, but didn't speak. One syllable would have broken her voice and spirit and she'd cry for the next hour. She could never do that in front of Pres, but she could *really* never do that in front of Mary Ellen.

In some ways, Melon was an Iron Maiden. Never would Mary Ellen show what bothered her. Kerry had never seen Mary Ellen flustered, let alone weeping. Melon was above the common run of human emotion. Usually Kerry did not know whether to envy this or not. Today she envied. Would that she could stalk through life without being upset by anything!

The boys talked exclusively of basketball.

Kerry had lost interest in the entire sport. In her opinion the season was too long. How nice that nobody cheered for baseball. Pres would be at rest, and she and Pres could concentrate on each other instead of school sports. With her luck, though, Pres would decide to go out for baseball, and she'd spend the entire spring clapping when he made a run and commiserating when he didn't. She felt dishonest at times, dishonest to herself, but she ignored the feeling and played the game Pres wanted.

Sports. Yuk, she thought dismally.

The sweater was as lovely as she had known it would be. Would Felicia Tilford buy something ugly? Of course not.

Rotten, rotten woman, Kerry thought. She said to Pres, "It's beautiful, Pres. You can't say you never get anything but socks and batteries. Not when your mother does something as thoughtful as this. And it fits you perfectly."

I am a saint, she told herself. Kerry, the Pure and Good.

Pres beamed, abandoning the topic of sweaters and going back to basketball.

So Kerry had made her choice. To keep peace in the Tilford family rather than tell Pres the ugly truth: The purchase of that sweater was not a gift for Pres. It was a slap for Kerry.

She felt curiously peaceful.

She had done the right thing. It wasn't fun. It wouldn't become fun. Especially tonight when she would look at the all-but-done-sweater in her bedroom. But she felt good about herself for doing it.

Ardith Engborg had been sitting with Mrs. Evans for twenty-five minutes, but it felt like two lifetimes. It was a miracle that Olivia had grown up sane. With a mother like this, a father who never spoke up, and all those earlier health problems, how had Olivia become such a fine girl?

Ardith said, "Mrs. Evans, if I thought for one minute that Olivia was endangering her life, I would not allow the cheers to be choreographed like that. I agree that these cheers are dangerous in comparison to ordinary sideline cheers, but they are not life-threatening."

"I am taking Olivia off the squad unless these dangerous stunts are eliminated," Mrs. Evans said implacably.

Ardith could argue no more. She had repeated herself enough. Mrs. Evans had the right and Ardith could not stop her. So on the final two games, the most important two games, there would be not six but five Varsity members. Nothing could be done but the most ordinary of cheers, because every single good routine required the perfect placement of each of the six, and each worked in precision with the others — depending on them, needing them.

All they'll be able to do is stand there and yell go, team, go, and wave a pompon or two, Ardith thought miserably.

Of course, there was a way out. She could agree to Mrs. Evans' terms. The kids would have to skip the spectacular routines Olivia and Mary Ellen had designed.

Which meant Garrison would outshine them totally.

Here they had raised the spirit of the entire school with carefully circulated rumors about how fantastic their cheers were going to be . . . and they would be depressingly, appallingly ordinary.

Ardith hated to lose as much as any high school kid.

Most of all, she did not want to be known as the coach of a *formerly* good squad.

They'll be destroyed, Ardith thought. They can't survive any more scorn. This, on top of Nancy's defection! How will my kids deal with it?

"All right," she told Mrs. Evans. "But you must come to the practice after school and tell the squad yourself."

If Ardith hoped this would deter Mrs. Evans, she was mistaken. Mrs. Evans relished the opportunity of telling those silly cheerleaders her daughter was associating with just what she thought of their so-called sport.

That afternoon, six kids gathered.

Pres was in a better mood than usual. It was rare for him to be on good terms with his parents and it made him lighthearted. He had no idea his emotions were a gift from Kerry.

Mary Ellen, having stayed in the hall until the last second — embracing Donny, stroking his lovely hair, posturing next to his large fine body — was soaring with pleasure. Angie was her usual sweet, distracted self. Walt was quiet, but seemingly happy, though one never knew anything about Walt's feelings. Nancy was hesitant, unsure — as well she might be, Ardith thought grimly. She did not know who she was angrier at right now — Mrs. Evans or Nancy.

And then there was Olivia.

Frozen in space. Fury and apprehension destroying the pretty features. Olivia knew better than anybody what her mother was capable of, and one look at the smug expresion on her mother's face had told her the bad news.

Ardith wished she'd taken two aspirin. But then, she thought, I wouldn't feel good now even if I could be comatose through this whole weekend.

The six began their warm-ups. Each had a favorite series and each worked quietly without fanfare. Limbering up. Relaxing their muscles. Getting ready for the long afternoon. Not too long — they didn't want to exhaust themselves before the game.

Little did they know there was no worry about exhaustion. Once they obeyed Mrs. Evans, they would have precious few things to do anyhow.

Ardith could have wept.

Her beautiful, hard-working, kids!

Ardith blew her whistle. The six stopped their exercising and walked over to her. At the same moment, the gym doors opened. Donny Parrish walked in, crossing this gym on his way to the lockers for the final practice his basketball team would have. He was closely followed by Troy and by a group of girls including Kerry, who climbed quietly up the bleachers to watch. Donny waved at Mary Ellen, who beamed at him. Nobody paid attention to Nancy. Nancy stared at her sneakers.

Perhaps an audience would slow Mrs. Evans down.

But Mrs. Evans looked delighted. More people to listen to her low opinion of cheerleading.

"Mrs. Evans has something she would like to say to the squad," Ardith said. She stepped back, removing herself from whatever Mrs. Evans chose to announce.

Five kids sat Indian-style on the floor, patiently waiting. They looked like kids expecting a party to be announced, or special prizes, or perhaps monetary awards.

Olivia did not sit. She stood among the others, her small wiry body as tight as a fist. When she spoke, her words came out brittle and hard. She almost whispered, and it was like a hiss of rage.

"I won't have it!"

Nobody beyond the squad could have heard a

sound. But the squad could hear, and was shocked by the rage in Olivia's voice. None of them, not even Pres, would have addressed a parent like that.

"You've tried to run my life since I was a child," Olivia hissed at her mother. "Well, you can't any longer. This is *my* life. If I want to risk breaking an ankle, it's my choice. All sports have a degree of danger. Soccer, football, gymnastics, and cheerleading. Everything good contains risk. And you're not ruining this for us, Mother. *You are not!*"

Mrs. Evans stared at her daughter, then she turned and left the gym. The squad watched her go. Olivia shrugged. "Don't think that means she's given up. She'll be back."

CHAPTER

P res Tilford had had stage fright before, but nothing compared to this! His nerves rippled as if they were flexing their muscles. He ran through in his mind the routine he and Olivia were about to execute. He had to have just the right force behind the lift. Just the same stance as at practice. (Practice! Wow, that Evans woman was something. And he thought *he* had family problems. You had to admire Olivia settling things like that. Still, Pres didn't like the thought of Mrs. Evans seated directly behind Mary Ellen. What sort of depressing, frightening things might she be muttering in Mary Ellen's ear?)

If we don't do that first routine soon, I'm going to flip out, Pres thought. He tried to glare at

Mary Ellen, but cheerleaders don't glare, and standing in a row the way they were, leading an ordinary sideline cheer that kept Angie happy but irritated everybody else, it was impossible to catch Melon's eye.

The game was hardly worth glancing at. It was only Grove Hill. Grove Hill was a soccer town. That Tarenton would cream them in basketball was undisputed. But people had not particularly come for the basketball tonight. They had come to see the honor of Varsity cheerleading restored. The whole school knew about the new routines. Every kid who'd watched even a minute of practice had reported with awe what Olivia and Mary Ellen had worked up.

"Time-out!" The ref's whistle was immediately followed by the piercing electronic bullhorn, and the teams quit playing and ran to the bench.

Pres tensed, ready to run out.

Mary Ellen did nothing.

Nothing.

Grove Hill cheerleaders danced out, taking the empty floor, and proceeded to spend a long, fruitful time-out with *their* best cheer!

The fans on the Tarenton side looked resentfully at their squad.

Walt muttered to Pres, "What's going on here? Did Mrs. Evans pay off Mary Ellen?"

"I think adoration of Donny fried her brains," Pres said.

Olivia's mother looked happy. She was the

only one. Nobody could imagine what was going on. A second time-out came (basketball was sometimes an infuriating game for cheerleaders — you never knew when, or if, you could get on the court, and you had to take advantage of openings quickly) and *again* Mary Ellen let Grove Hill seize the opportunity.

"Listen to me," Olivia hissed. "We practiced a jillion hours in order to make a display out here, Mary Ellen. What is your problem? Why aren't you doing anything? What kind of captain are you, anyway?"

Ardith Engborg did not interfere. She sensed in Mary Ellen a fine control that the squad did not see. Mary Ellen had something up her sleeve, though what it could be, Ardith had no idea.

Mary Ellen simply ignored her squad. The action began again, and again they began their rather ordinary, familiar sideline cheers.

A *third* opportunity — and a *third* time Mary Ellen did nothing.

Even Angie was upset now, and it took a lot to get her angry. "Their captain even waited for you, Mary Ellen," she protested. "She knew it was our turn. She only went out when it was perfectly clear that you weren't going to make a move."

"This is not a game tonight," Mary Ellen said. "This is war. And this is my strategy."

"Some strategy," Olivia snorted. "We never do it at all. I love it, Mary Ellen. It's really exciting."

125

Mary Ellen tossed her lovely blonde hair. Before the game she had sprayed sparkle into the curls. It seemed that her whole personality glittered like her hair. She was unsurpassably lovely.

She caught even Donny's eye, as he waited for a Grove Hill player to attempt a foul shot.

Mary Ellen thought, How wonderful — his eyes are on me.

The crowd thought, How awful. He's putting romance ahead of the game he has to win. What if he does this tomorrow night against Ben Adamson and Garrison?

And Patrick, seeing Donny look at Mary Ellen, felt his heart turn over.

Mary Ellen said quietly, "We let Grove Hill go out there three times. Three times they do acceptable, ordinary routines. Then we go out. And we knock 'em dead. This gym is going to give us a standing ovation. You wait and see."

Nancy Goldstein had never heard of a standing ovation for cheerleaders. Or one at any kind of ball game. It seemed to her standing ovations were confined to musical concerts, or maybe Presidential candidates. But not cheerleaders at Grove Hill basketball games. However, Mary Ellen's strategy did sound reasonable.

Nancy wondered how Ben was doing in his game. She wondered what she was going to do tonight. Tomorrow night. And all the nights that stretched out there, filled with painful decisions.

* * *

In the bleachers, Kerry Elliot sat with two girl friends. During the third time-out when Grove Hill cheerleaders were once more boring everybody, and Mary Ellen once more enraging everybody, Kerry climbed over laps, legs, overcoats, and toddlers, down four rows and across twenty bodies, to where Mr. and Mrs. Tilford were sitting.

It was rare for Pres's parents to come to games. And this was a game against a weak team. Kerry did not know what had brought on this loyalty. Had Scotland wrought a change of heart in Mrs. Tilford? Had Pres begged them to come see him in the new routines?

Kerry sat down next to Mrs. Tilford and said gaily, "Hi, there! Isn't the game exciting?"

It was not exciting. Grove Hill was being beaten so solidly it was almost embarrassing.

"I'm no judge of basketball," Mrs. Tilford said, hardly glancing at Kerry.

"If this is typical opposition," Mr. Tilford said, looking with boredom at his watch, and then the scoreboard clock, "no wonder Tarenton is the reigning champion. How come our cheerleaders haven't done much of anything?"

"They're saving themselves," Kerry said.

"For what?" Mr. Tilford said irritably.

"Wait till you see Pres," Kerry said. "He's fantastic."

Mrs. Tilford looked uncomfortable.

127

Kerry could not hold back any longer. She had to find out. She said, "That was an absolutely lovely sweater you brought Pres, Mrs. Tilford." She looked right into Mrs. Tilford's eyes and smiled her sweetest smile.

Felicia Tilford flushed hotly.

I was right, Kerry thought. She did do it on purpose.

A scream rose up from the court. Grove Hill stole the ball, and proceeded to make one basket after another, until they were a mere two points behind. Tarenton, shocked out of its complacency, was going to have to fight after all! The game picked up in intensity. Fans began screaming. The Pompon Squad waved scarlet-and-white clouds of fluff and Varsity led the crowd in several throat-ruining cheers.

Kerry said, "We're all looking forward to the party tonight."

Mrs. Tilford shuddered. "I just hope there isn't any damage. I thought this party was just for the squad, but Pres informs me all those basketball players and their girl friends and all these other kids will be there. They look like a rowdy bunch to me."

"Don't worry about them," Kerry said. "I'll make sure nobody does a thing. All they want to do is stand around and eat and tell each other how brilliantly they all did, anyhow."

Mrs. Tilford made no comment.

Kerry had to decide if she really wanted to

win Pres's parents over, or if she wanted to join Mrs. Tilford in some sort of backstage play of being rude to each other. Mrs. Tilford isn't very grown-up, Kerry thought.

She went back to her girl friends.

Halftime.

The score was Tarenton, thirty-three; Grove Hill, thirty-one.

The basketball teams trotted off to their locker rooms.

Fans began to think in terms of Coke and Pepsi, popcorn and hot dogs.

Ardith Engborg put a loud, rhythmic rock tape on the loudspeaker system.

Mary Ellen led the Varsity Squad out for the halftime display.

People were getting up to go outdoors and have a cigarette. Little children were begging for money to buy snacks. Friends were shouting across rows of people to greet each other. Mittens and scarves were falling under the bleachers and nine-year-old boys were scrambling underneath to rescue them.

People watched with half an eye as the squad lined up. Halftime was background. Like piped-in music in an elevator. Action to gossip by, or sip a cold drink by. It was filler before the game began again.

And then the new routine started.

Vibrant, demanding splashes of scarlet and white.

Strong leg movements, sharp geometric arm movements.

The fine smiles on six handsome faces.

The swirl of pompons, the grace of flared skirts, the strength of the boys' lifts.

The crowd quieted. The flow to the exits ceased.

Mary Ellen had the crowd in the palm of her hand. Her timing was perfect. Just when they had hundreds of eyes upon them, they would move into the spectacular part of Olivia's design. The music throbbed. The beat intensified. This routine had no words, no actual cheering — it was a *display*.

And display they did.

Olivia leaped in front of the squad, and swerved dramatically in a series of eye-catching movements. The other five slipped gracefully to new positions. Olivia ran to the far end of the gym, her small, light body the picture of feminine strength and beauty.

Pres's throat tightened. He bent slightly and cupped his hands. He forgot Kerry, his parents, the crowd. He thought of nothing but the motion to come, which had to be exactly right.

Olivia straightened, holding herself dramatically. Hundreds of people frowned slightly, not sure what to expect, but sure that it was something special. They knew by the way this little girl stood, by her confidence and excited features. Olivia ran. With breathtaking speed she launched herself at Pres, landing with one slender foot in his cupped hands, her fingertips grazing his shoulder for support as she rose. He thrust her into the air. She spun like a nymph over the heads of the other cheerleaders, landing effortlessly yards beyond them. The crowd gasped. Before they could think of clapping, the squad reversed positions and repeated the maneuver from the opposite side.

Then Mary Ellen and Olivia both burst out from the squad, like matching bombshells — except that one was small and wiry, the other golden and sparkling. They exploded in a series of cartwheels and flips that brought the crowd to its feet. Just as Mary Ellen and Olivia landed in front of the others, Pres and Walt lifted Nancy to their shoulders. Nancy flung out a pair of huge fluffy pompons and laughed at the skylights. Angie leaped with arched back and neatly curved legs to land in front of them all, the most angelic smile in Tarenton decorating the squad like a star in the sky.

For one moment the Varsity Squad remained there: frozen in time. And then the crowd began to clap — wild, thunderous clapping and foot stomping and cheering. Whistles came from the boys in the back who could pierce eardrums with their pursed lips.

"Tarenton! Tarenton! Tarenton!" they screamed over and over.

Mary Ellen broke formation first, and the others followed her lead. They had never practiced such a thing, but when Mary Ellen made a sudden sweeping bow, the others did, too, and the applause rose to even greater heights. Hands resting lightly on their waists, the squad ran lightly off the floor, as if they had never exercised at all. They reached their bench at the exact moment that the teams emerged from their locker rooms for the warm-ups.

Patrick and Kerry felt the same emotions as they looked at Mary Ellen and Pres: pride and excitement and overwhelming love. Vanessa Barlow narrowed her eyes as she stared at the squad, and felt that she had never hated six people so much in all her life . . . and Vanessa knew what hatred was.

Mrs. Evans let out a long breath. She felt as if she had not breathed in hours. She had been suspended in the space of her anxiety.

But Olivia is wonderful! she thought, astonished. I knew she was wonderful, of course. She's my daughter. But I didn't know she was *that* wonderful.

Nancy Goldstein was so tired she could hardly sit up straight. And so proud she could burst. *We did it!* We showed them. Mary Ellen said we would and she was right!

"Olivia, you were so perfect," Mary Ellen whispered, hugging Olivia fiercely.

Olivia was not good at accepting praise. "There's no such thing as *so* perfect," she scolded. "Either you're perfect or you're not."

"You are," Pres said, and he kissed her forehead. Now that they had done the routine in public once, his fears were gone. Tomorrow night against Garrison he'd be tense, but not terrified.

Mary Ellen really was an excellent captain. Pres hadn't realized it until now. She was calm, calculating, like a general at war. And she'd won.

He looked past the squad, searching the bleachers for Kerry. He spotted her at last, directly behind him, up six rows. She was smiling that cherished smile that made him feel so good. Kerry saluted him to tell him how well he'd done.

He could hardly wait for the party. He waved to her once more and turned his attention to the upcoming second half. He did not look for his parents. It had not occurred to him that they would have come.

Angie hugged Mary Ellen, hugged Olivia, hugged Nancy and Walt and Pres. Nancy hugged everybody right back. *Never* had she felt so important, so much a part of a truly fine piece of work.

From behind them the Tarenton fans called out praise. For this moment, the crowd was not composed of basketball fans — but of cheerleading fans. Nancy thought she would burst with pride.

And then she thought of Ben.

And anxiety gripped her as fiercely as the joy of a moment before. She was part of a wonderful group, and they gave her a lot, as she gave to them. What did Ben have to equal that?

CHAPTER

11

Rarely had Tarenton High emptied so fast. Exhilarated by their victory and the sight of their wonderful cheerleaders, Tarenton kids abandoned the building for their various celebrations. There was the Burger House crowd, the Pizza Parlor crowd, the going-home-and-lonely crowd, and there was the partying-at-Pres-Tilford's crowd.

Nancy was not a member of any.

The thrill of success vanished in quivers of nervousness. The joy of the teenagers around her — the pummeling and shouting and congratulating — seemed to have nothing to do with her. *What am I doing?* she thought. *Why am I standing here alone?*

I'm doing this for Ben.

Sometimes the face you most want to picture is the most elusive. Nancy tried to summon up an image of Ben, to comfort herself that she was doing what was important to her. But she could not seem to remember Ben. She had a vague sense of his bulk, and that was all. She could not feel his personality, recall his looks.

Nancy could not make herself go out on the front steps of the school and find her parents, who were driving her over to the Burger House to meet Ben. It seemed an irrevocable step, which would lead to terrifying things, painful things, lonely things.

She pretended to herself that she had forgotten something in the girls' locker room, and walked swiftly back, trying to look purposeful. Several faces studied her, and she thought the looks were ones of scorn and dislike: that they knew all about her, traitor that she was, and a sick taste rose in her throat.

Mary Ellen was brushing her hair. Tiny sparklets of gold and silver shivered momentarily in the air as the stiff bristles pulled through her thick, lovely blonde hair. Mary Ellen stood in her pale blue bra and pants in front of the full-length mirror and admired herself. She kept tossing her head lightly, so that the shining hair trembled on her shoulders and slipped across her soft skin. She thought of Donny, and how brilliant he had been tonight, and would be in the future, and she thought of herself at his side. And then she thought of Patrick. She tried not to compare Donny to him, knowing which one would sweep through her heart. Mary Ellen, she thought, why are you so superficial?

She slipped into a pair of deep green, almost black, cords and belted them with a leather sash. Then three layers of shirting, deftly tugging the collar and cuffs of each layer, running her fingers under her hair and flicking it up and out. It fell back on her shoulders, glistening.

And now the party. Pres's house. The mansion on the lake, with all its wonderful large, dark rooms and their deep, imperious colors. What a house for romance! She saw herself falling onto one of the plush velvet sofas under the ancestral portraits with their intricate gold frames, lying there with Donny.

And then, in the mirror, she saw Nancy Goldstein.

Mary Ellen's lips tightened with annoyance.

Nancy was making a big mistake. Pretty soon Nancy would destroy her Tarenton existence and what would she have to show for it? Not much: a hulking basketball star who would graduate and go on to other things that wouldn't include Nancy.

Well, if she acted like that, Nancy didn't deserve anything good anyhow. True, Nancy had worked wonderfully tonight, as hard as the rest. Varsity had been six people as one, and Mary Ellen was proud of her squad. But that did not cancel the fact that Nancy was going to go out with Ben Adamson.

Nancy was silent, and Mary Ellen did not speak to her. Two girls who worked intimately every single day, for the same cause, and neither acknowledged the other's presence.

Mary Ellen's faith in her own beauty was marred. Nancy was so lovely in such a different way: dark, mysterious, curvaceous. Right now clad in a dark crimson sweater the color of Pres's formal parlor.

I hate her, Mary Ellen thought. She left the locker room without talking to Nancy, and so did everybody else there. Only Angie whispered, in a flute-like voice, "Bye, Nance."

Nancy's chin quivered.

Good, Mary Ellen thought. I hope she cries, and her mascara runs and her eyes get red and her cheeks get all blotchy. Traitor.

"We'll miss you at Pres's," Angie said gently.

We will not, Mary Ellen thought.

Donny had showered and changed faster than Mary Ellen, which came as no surprise. Almost anybody on earth could shower and change faster than Mary Ellen Kirkwood. Of course, most people didn't have as much fun looking in the mirror, either. Furthermore, Mary Ellen loved to make people wait for her. It made her feel powerful. And it was so much more fun to walk into waiting arms, rather than leaning on a wall waiting for the body to emerge.

They were the focus of all eyes. There was nothing — *nothing* — that Mary Ellen loved more than to be watched when she looked her very best. Against her will, she found herself looking surreptitiously beyond Donny to see if Patrick was also watching.

And there he was, true to form, standing in the back of the press of kids. Their eyes met. Patrick was calm, a small, knowing smile on his face. Mary Ellen swept her lashes in her sexiest way. Donny thought the message was for him. Carefully Mary Ellen did not look Patrick's way again, but that one moment when their eyes had locked had rocked her. She left the school with Donny, casually offering Angie a ride to Pres's with them.

Angie accepted with a sigh.

Pain at seeing the affection between Donny and Mary Ellen chewed at Angie. She had a much deeper affection for Marc than Mary Ellen had ever had for *any* boy, but Marc was not there. She was beginning to wonder if he would ever be there again. College was much harder for him this semester and Marc was broke and having to work extra hours, with the result that Angie rarely saw him. At times her life was painfully lonely, which was absurd, because Angie was more in love than any of them. All very well to have a wonderful boyfriend, but an absentee boyfriend could be an equal agony to not having one at all.

But it was not in Angie to complain.

Cheerfully she greeted Donny, congratulating

him, careful to remember each of his spectacular baskets and steals. She got in the backseat alone, grateful that the ride to Pres's house was short.

Nancy Goldstein was left alone in the locker room.

She straightened her collar several times and questioned the wisdom of wearing that particular necklace. But there was no jewelry box here in the locker room. She was stuck with what she'd chosen. Was she too dressy? Such vivid colors! Nancy looked her best in bright things, but now she felt as conspicuous as fireworks on a black night.

She left the locker room shaking, but there was no need. Her friends and fellow students had left several moments before, and the hallways were almost deserted. She did not have to face the questioning looks of a single person. Her parents were waiting by the door and it was just a question of walking in the dark to their car.

Kerry could not imagine what was taking Pres so long. As usual, the two boy cheerleaders used the same locker room as the basketball team. (They could hardly go into the girls' locker room with Nancy, Angie, Olivia, and Mary Ellen, although they generally asked to do so!) But Pres was the swiftest of dressers. Much to his mother's disgust, Pres took few pains with his appearance. He was sufficiently good-looking to get away with this, tugging on old jeans, half buttoning an old shirt (skipping the buttons that didn't show), and pulling on a sweater that more than likely had torn elbows. Then he'd run a comb through his dark-blond hair and call it quits. Sixty seconds max.

Sighing, Kerry walked in a circuit of the front halls, wondering where Pres could be. Most of the team had already left for his house, and Mr. and Mrs. Tilford had left literally before the game was over. They'd taken a position at the door and when it was clear that Tarenton really would win, had walked out, missing the final cheers and screaming. They were obviously nervous over this party. Probably had visions of drunken kids hanging from the chandeliers. There were a few who would do that, given the chance but since everybody wanted Pres to give another party, they were going to be careful at this one. Very careful. Even Pres would be careful.

Kerry was not exactly annoyed that Pres hadn't come out. It took a lot to annoy Kerry. She did wish, however, that he would hurry up. He was probably telling silly locker room jokes to the other boys. He'd want to wrap that up before he joined her. He was meticulously careful to speak and behave in a gentlemanly fashion around Kerry. If Mrs. Tilford had liked Kerry, Kerry would have shared the joke with her. Kerry told plenty of locker room jokes with the girls, but she was equally carefully to maintain a pristine, pure front for Pres! It was funny, really.

When Pres still hadn't come out five minutes later, Kerry was so restless she hiked down another corridor. This is just what Nancy Goldstein did, Kerry thought, giggling to herself. And look what happened to her! A sex god caught up to her.

Well, Kerry already had a sex god in her life, and he'd better catch up to her or he was going to be a sex god in big trouble.

Unlike Nancy, Kerry was afraid of pitch dark, so she didn't take the final corner, but turned at the EXIT sign to go back to the front foyer. And there was Pres, flying toward her, running as fast as he could in his eagerness to join her. She was faintly surprised he could even see her — it was so dim and her clothing so dark — but perhaps he'd seen her in the distance walking this way and just knew she was down the hall somewhere.

Pres leaped, ran right up the side of the wall, grunting slightly. His shoes made slick, hard, rubery sounds and left black patches on the wall that she could see even in the dark like ghosts in reverse against the white paint.

"Pres Tilford!" Kerry screamed, absolutely infuriated. "How *could* you! You stupid, dumb idiot. I can't believe it!"

She ran toward him, intending to grab him by the shoulders and shake him until his teeth rattled — no matter that he was six inches taller and heaven knew how many pounds heavier than she. At a time like this! To jeopardize everything

142

— from the Varsity Squad, to the party, to the victory tomorrow, to his entire school career! Just to show off for her!

It took a lot to annoy Kerry Elliot, and this was a lot.

Shrieking her rage, she rushed up to him. Shadows filled the hall. The face before her was a pale blot in the dark. She had the weirdest sensation of being *afraid* of Pres. Her fingers brushed his sleeve, and the fabric was slicker than anything Pres would wear. "Pres?" she said hesitantly. The arms she had touched came up in her face violently, shoving her, and Kerry cried out in pain and fear, staggering backward and hitting her head against the stone-hard tile walls of the corridor.

"Wonderful game, dear," Mr. Goldstein said. Nancy didn't feel like talking about it.

"Brilliant cheering," her mother said.

Nancy didn't say anything to that either. Her breath was coming shorter and shorter. What if Ben didn't come? What if she had to sit alone in Burger House for hours waiting? What if his game lasted much longer than theirs had? What if he didn't feel like making the drive to Tarenton after all? What if he wasn't very trustworthy to begin with and hadn't really planned on coming anyway?

"Weren't you proud of yourselves?" her mother asked anxiously.

"Oh, yes," Nancy said mechanically.

Her parents exchanged worried looks.

They arrived at the Burger House. Nancy's heart sank even more. A swarm of Tarenton kids — not her crowd, really, but classmates — was pouring into the place, greeting even more Tarenton kids.

I can't handle it, she thought.

It was like the first day of school after she moved here. Sheer, raw panic. *Mommy-take-me-home* type panic.

Nancy peered into the parking lot. The moment she saw Ben, she remembered why she was sacrificing. He was so attractive! He parked, and got slowly out of his car, unfolding his length, and when he had shut the door behind him, he stretched his body, yawned slightly, and looked up at the stars.

Nancy grinned to herself. "Bye, Mom . . . Dad," she said easily, happily. "See you later." She jumped out of her parents' car to go to him. Ben had already seen her. He did not move to greet her but waited, like some carved statue, for her to come to him. The instant she got there he took her arm and escorted her toward the restaurant door.

Panic swept over Nancy again. "I thought we were going to Garrison for a party there."

"We are. I'm thirsty, though. Got to get a Coke before we start driving. You want something?"

I want not to go in there, Nancy thought. She

slowed down, so that Ben was practically dragging her, but he sensed nothing, or else her weight was so minor that there was nothing to sense.

Into the Burger House they walked. Among basketball fans. Groups celebrating the Tarenton win. Kids who hated Garrison. Whose talk was of nothing but tomorrow's smashing of Ben Adamson.

With a soft, muffled thump, the door closed behind them. It was not soft enough that nobody noticed their entry. Ben was too large to go unnoticed, no matter how softly he moved. Nancy, clad in scarlet, decorated him like a shining ball on a Christmas tree.

He loves this, she thought, looking up at him. He can feel the anger we're arousing, and he loves it. She was terribly aware that she was being led in, on his arm, not just walking in with him. Nobody hissed at her.

But they wanted to.

Never had service seemed so slow, or the filling of a paper cup so time-consuming. Nancy thought perhaps an hour had gone by as they stood there. Ben counted out his change with maddening slowness. She refused his offer of a drink for the third time. When he finally turned to leave, he surveyed the restaurant from his extra height in a lordly way, refusing to be hurried or worried.

I would never go into enemy territory, she thought. But he loves doing it. That's what this is all about. I'm his ticket into the fray.

It was a relief to be back in his car! The door slammed behind her, the lock pushed down, the seat belt securing her. It was like a medieval castle — impregnable, entirely safe from the raging eyes of the peasants who hated the lord.

Ben talked about his basketball game. They had won, of course. From Ben's voice this was never in any doubt. He felt totally ready for tomorrow night, he told her. He was in perfect shape, had the perfect attitude. There was no doubt whatsoever about the outcome of the fight against her Tarenton.

She pulled her jacket a little tighter.

It occurred to her that in fact she *was* about to do what Ben had just done. She *was* going into enemy territory. On Ben's arm. Like a piece of Ben's property.

She screamed.

The sound of her own scream was more horrifying to Kerry than the blow on her face. It was a dreadful noise, scraping her nerve, rasping out of her throat like some evil late-night movie.

Her head hurt. It had all happened too fast to be sure of anything. She could not really even tell whether she *was* hurt, or just terrified. The hall echoed with her scream and her head ached in response.

There was a commotion at the other end of the hall: people scrambling, yelling, demanding to know where the light switches were. A second scream stayed in Kerry's throat, choking her.

The vandal, she realized. Not Pres, but the vandal.

She had to notice him. She had to make some intelligent observations so they could catch him, not let Pres be blamed. But she knew nothing. She had seen nothing. A blurred whiteness at the right height for a face. Slippery fabric.

Her face was wet and she realized that she was crying.

The vandal's feet were slamming into the floor as he raced to the dark back of the building. He can't get out, she reassured herself. It's locked.

And then she remembered that the whole purpose of EMERGENCY EXITs was to be able to get out in an emergency. The kid would vanish into the night and nobody would know anything more about him except that it was not a good idea to interrupt him at work.

"Where are the lights?" came a yell.

"It's Kerry!" screamed somebody else.

"She got mugged or something!"

"There he goes! Somebody catch him!"

And then Pres's arms were around her. They closed in comfort, and almost immediately opened with his need to run after her attacker. She could feel his mixed rage and love in that single clasp. "I'm not really hurt," she said, without knowing if this was true or not. "I'm just scared."

The lights came on.

Pres looked her over like a father would his

newborn child. Was she all there? Was she well formed? His hands ran over her face, and then over the back of her head, and light as his touch was, she winced. She had really slammed into that tile wall.

"We got him!" came the chorus of voices from the end of the hall.

The adults arrived by then: the principal, the vice-principal, a few parents, one of the assistant coaches, and the two cops who were always assigned to high school games.

The only other girl still there was Susan Yardley, one of Nancy Goldstein's friends. Even in the horror of the moment, Kerry had time to feel sorry for Nancy, because Susan had all but ended the friendship when she saw Nancy with Ben. Susan's family was Old Tarenton, and people who consorted with Garrison stars might as well be dead.

"But who is he?" Susan said blankly, staring at the culprit the boys were dragging back down the hall.

"Some sophomore," her boyfriend said grimly. "Dill is his last name."

"Jimmy Dill,"' Pres said, astonished. "He's in my gym class."

They stared at Jimmy Dill.

He was pitiful. Tall, but scrawny. Not good-looking at all — not a hope of ever being good-looking, either. Acne and an ugly nose and fat lips. Now that they had him pinned by the arms, the boys had no idea what to do with him. They felt uncomfortable, as if they were the ones doing something wrong. Jimmy Dill seemed like such an unlikely person to be the source of trouble.

The principal turned to Kerry. "Are you hurt?" she said.

Kerry saw instantly that Jimmy Dill would be in a lot more trouble if she were. He had meant only to ruin the walls — he had not known some girl would attack him in the dark, grabbing his arm. She would have a swelling on the back of her head, but that was it. She said, "No. Just scared. I didn't need to scream."

They accepted this. Kerry thought, *Am I wrong?* Is Jimmy Dill a vicious person and I'm going to be partially responsible because I let him go?

"Let's go," mumbled the other kids. "Come on, Pres. Let's go to your party."

Jimmy Dill seemed so frightened. So pitiable. They could not bear to look at him.

The kids left. The adults could handle Jimmy Dill. They wanted only to walk away and pretend they had nothing to do with the whole thing. How grateful they were to be kids who felt they had something to offer — anything at all — more than Jimmy did, who felt he was nothing. As a group, they shuddered.

How strange it was to come out into a parking lot filled with kids who had not yet left for Pres's house: leaning on their cars, dancing, clowning, yelling, singing and clapping. High spirits filled the entire school grounds. What a contrast to the disaster inside.

"All right, Pres!" they shouted like a cheer, although Pres was the only cheerleader there. "Let's *go!*"

Everybody loves a party, and even more if it's at somebody else's house, and the somebody else is rich and will have terrific food and unlimited space and every single record or cassette anybody ever wanted to dance to.

Some citizens of Tarenton might have thought they felt an earthquake tremor. Mild shocks seemed to travel across the asphalt.

But it was just the basketball team headed toward Fable Point and the Tilford mansion.

Jimmy Dill was forgotten.

CHAPTER

Nancy Goldstein was sick with dismay. She could taste it, and she quivered with it as if she had fever from the flu.

She had no idea who might be the host or hostess at this party. Ben had led her into an unknown house in an unknown neighborhood, where he was welcomed with screams of delight, much pounding on the back from the boys, and lots of giggling kisses from pretty girls.

"And who's this?" they all exclaimed. From the way they frowned at her, Nancy knew they half recognized her, but couldn't place her.

"This is Nancy," Ben said simply, giving no details. His arm remained around her so that she was protected from the onslaught of Garrison kids.

"Oh, my *God*!" screamed a Garrison girl, and then burst into half-crazed laughter. "She's a rah-rah from Tarenton. I know her. Look at this, everybody. Benny's brought a rah-rah from Tarenton!"

They gathered around as if Ben had brought a trained chimpanzee.

"I give you credit, Ben," one of his fellow basketball players said. "You not only steal every ball they try to play — you steal their little rah-rah as well."

"She's kind of cute," another boy said, as if Nancy weren't standing within two inches of him.

"Do a cheer for us," said a snickering voice from a girl wearing a fan cap in Garrison colors. "Come on. Do that silly little 'All the Way' cheer for little old Tarenton."

"And does she, Ben?" said the basketball player, digging him in the ribs.

"Does she what?" Ben said innocently.

"Go all the way."

They laughed uproariously. Ben hugged Nancy to his side with such intimacy that anybody would have figured they'd been sleeping together for months. I won't cry, Nancy thought. I won't cry.

Ben led her across that room and several more until they came to a huge buffet. It was a very adult setup: casseroles and fancy finger foods. Nothing like the plain old chips and dip that

Nancy was used to. Gradually she realized, from the number of adults present, that this was a fund raiser. These were alumni, coaches, athletic boosters, parents, and teams.

And I'm part of it! she thought. I'm providing some of the entertainment!

Nancy could not see a single nice person in the crowd. She knew this was ridiculous. Garrison had to have as many nice people per capita as Tarenton. But the room was jammed with staring kids who thought it was the biggest joke in the world that Ben Adamson had snared a Tarenton rah-rah.

And how snide they were about cheerleading.

It was clear that in Garrison, if you were a cheerleader, you were a stupid, sex-crazed airhead. Good for nothing, except maybe going all the way on a Saturday night.

She prayed for support from Ben, but he gave none. For one thing, he was literally unreachable. He was too tall. She had to crook her neck to look into his face, and without fail his eyes were crisscrossing the room, checking out the composition of the party, catching eyes and accepting congratulations and adulation.

For another thing, she really did not know the boy at all. She had no idea how to confess to him that she felt rotten. That she was embarrassed, humiliated even.

He was unaware of her discomfort.

He felt no discomfort, and it apparently did not occur to him that her perspective would be different.

He would not protect her from these gawking, gossiping people. She was on her own. The faces around her blurred, as if she was underwater and they were leering down at her through murky liquid.

She yearned for Tarenton and her friends and her roots and her squad with an intensity that almost made her weep. Here she was on the arm of this splendid boy . . . and she was excruciatingly lonely.

Finally they left the brightly lit buffet and returned to one of the inner rooms, where it was darker, and there was some dancing. Nancy loved to dance. I'll unwind when we dance, she thought. I'll be okay. I won't disintegrate.

But he didn't dance. He took her to a couch in the corner. There was already a couple there wrapped in each other's arms, sprawled out and taking up most of the space. If she had known the kids — or known Ben, for that matter — Nancy would have made wisecracks. But tonight it made her supremely uncomfortable. Ben obviously expected her to cooperate in the same way. *All the way.* Next to a pair of Garrison strangers who were ninety percent there already.

Ben cupped her face in his hands and kissed her.

What do I do? she thought. I don't know Ben

at all. And I don't want to get to know him sexually before we've had a single real conversation!

It was a wonderful kiss.

Nancy burst into tears.

Ben jerked back as if they had burned him. He stared at her, totally thrown, with no idea what to do next. He was not the only one. Nancy Goldstein had no idea what to do next either.

She was at a crossroads. In Tarenton her best friends, her squad, were partying without her. In Garrison she sat in the arms of a tall, dark, mysterious stranger of whom every girl dreams. But how worthwhile was the dream? Parts of it appeared to be nightmare.

Nancy ached for Ben. Momentarily she considered following the example of the other couple. But she ached even more for life as she had known it only a few days before: safe, warm, welcoming, and friendly.

"Ben," she said huskily, "take me home."

"I've heard that line before," he said. "It doesn't worry me."

"I *mean* it, Ben. Please."

"Aw, come on, Nancy. This is fun."

If he weren't so exciting to her, it would be easy, she thought. If our teams weren't competing, it would be easy. If I didn't love Tarenton so much, it would be easy.

But it's not easy. Nothing about this is easy.

"Please take me home."

Ben ignored her.

New panic seized her. What if she *couldn't* get home? What if the decision had already been made for her, by someone who was stronger enough and heavier enough to choose whatever he wanted, *whenever* he wanted it?

"Ben, I made a mistake."

"Not yet. Mistakes are yet to come. You're doing fine." He brushed away the few tears and kissed her cheeks.

"Ben, I'm not kidding. This party is a mistake for me. I don't belong here. I shouldn't have come. Please take me home."

"You expect me to abandon a party in my honor? When you're my date?"

If only she had an ally with her! Some girl, some parent, some friend, who would help her! "Ben," Nancy said, "I know this is rude. You're a wonderful person and I wish things were different, but they're not. I shouldn't be at a Garrison party. It makes me feel sick. I want to go home and cheer for Tarenton. I like you very much. I want you, too. But tomorrow night I want Tarenton winning, not you, and I can't bear to be here another minute."

She had certainly put that strongly enough.

She could not look up at him.

But if the definition of a champion is being a good loser, then Ben Adamson truly was a champion. He did not want Nancy to cry. He did not want to be the reason for any tears, especially in public, on his turf, where he was being watched.

He took Nancy back to his car, amid scores of wisecracks that they all knew what would be going on in the backseat of *that* car, and without argument drove her the several miles to Tarenton.

They talked very little.

Nancy was drained. It seemed a miracle she could even sit there, let alone attempt to be witty and interesting.

As for Ben, it was his policy not to consider failures. He considered, instead, the game coming up, and the strategy he would use to destroy Donny Parrish, the only hope of Tarenton Varsity Basketball.

"Are you sorry you got mixed up with me?" Nancy asked.

Ben had already forgotten her. He was concentrating on driving, which he loved, and the game to come, which he intended to win. "No, I'm not sorry," he said. "You're a lovely girl. And you're making the right decision." No use having an enemy where he might someday want a friend. He smiled at her.

It seemed to please her. She relaxed.

Ben thought briefly of Wendy, the girl he had lined up as his next candidate. His thoughts returned more quickly to Donny. Donny had a tendency to get angry and make judgments without enough thought behind them. A regrettable tendency Ben intended to exploit.

"Turn left here," Nancy said.

Ben thought it must be another route to her

157

house and obeyed her. They ended up, however, at a road he'd never seen before.

Fable Point. Private, the signs said.

"Where's this?" Ben said, confused.

"The party I should have gone to in the first place. Listen, I'm sorry."

"No hard feelings." Ben leaned toward her.

She yearned to kiss him good-bye, but she knew if she kissed him once — felt that rough cheek, touched that rough hair — she would knuckle under. Tell him, Forget Tarenton. Drive into a deserted lane somewhere and we'll go all the way.

But she got out of the car instead, waved, and began walking, before Ben could swing the car around to go back to Garrison. She knew he had forgotten her already. She only hoped she could forget him as easily. Nobody in Tarenton could compare, except Donny, and that comparison was not in Donny's favor.

She went down the dark lane toward Pres's house.

Every light in the huge place was lit. Even in winter with storm doors and windows tightly caulked she could hear the party raging. Silhouettes of kids appeared in most of the windows. Cold though it was, there was a bunch of them on the lovely front porch that swept around the mansion in circles. The kids were laughing. When Nancy walked in out of the dark, one of the boys exclaimed, "Where did you come from?"

"Just passing through," she said, going inside.

The foyer was empty.

The huge, formal front parlor was empty.

She passed the pictures of Tilford ancestors and followed the gallery where a grandfather clock collection ticked mercilessly and an antique harpsichord collected dust.

In front of her was the huge addition Felicia Tilford had designed: the enormous family room with the great glass walls that faced Narrow Brook Lake.

The room was filled with her friends. With noise and laughter and music and the wonderful smell of good hot food.

Oh, please take me back! Nancy thought. *Let me be one of the crowd. Forget Ben. Please, please.*

Only one face looked up.

Mary Ellen.

Her captain, her fellow cheerleader, her friend.

Mary Ellen frowned and turned her back.

CHAPTER

 13

Donny Parrish had no sooner won the game against Grove Hill, than he began to get keyed up about the game against Garrison on Saturday.

He stood in the middle of Pres Tilford's magnificent family room (the Tilfords called it the Lake Room, because its huge glass walls had such a fine view of Narrow Brook Lake) and tried to pay attention to Mary Ellen.

I should go home and get ten hours of sleep, Donny thought. He knew perfectly well he was so wired up he wouldn't be able to fall asleep until dawn anyhow.

He felt he should eat red meat, drink a gallon of orange juice, and swallow a mess of spinach. He reached for a bowl of taco chips and another Pepsi.

There was slow music on the stereo and Mary Ellen wanted to dance. Donny could not possibly dance slowly. His muscles were a jangle. There was nothing slow, calm, or smooth in his entire body or mind. He said to her, "Next fast one, okay?"

She was so lovely! How lucky he was to have Mary Ellen Kirkwood. Donny knew he had her only because he was a basketball star. He was glad he was tall and well coordinated. Mary Ellen wouldn't be caught dead with a short klutz. Mary Ellen chattered away and Donny didn't listen. He could think only of Ben Adamson. Ben's added height was a tremendous asset to Garrison. There was no way for Donny to beat that. And Ben's personality wasn't exactly a liability, either. Donny couldn't make up his mind about Ben. Was all that strutting an act, or was it the real Ben?

"Now it's a fast one," Mary Ellen said, and she jumped up, pulling on his hand. Donny didn't resist. He rather liked fast dances. It took up energy. You would think after an exhausting game he'd be out of energy, but instead he had even more of it. Mary Ellen sang the lyrics under her breath. She didn't have a voice to speak of, but she memorized the lyrics to all the songs she loved and whispered along rhythmically.

They danced vibrantly, bodies swerving and turning, jabbing and thrusting across the floor space. What a house Pres had! Donny's family was well off, too. His parents owned a restaurant and worked long, exhausting hours. But even the restaurant had nothing to compare with the dance floor Pres could offer. It was amazing. Like another world.

As the pulsing rhythm took over his body, Donny relaxed. He could enjoy Mary Ellen again. How he loved that golden hair! And her wonderful smile. Directed at *him*. Mary Ellen was always up when she was with him. It was one reason Donny liked her so much. Oh, sure, there was the usual stuff about her looks, and how sexy she was. But Donny liked a team person. Someone to carry the ball and not complain if she got stepped on. Although Donny could not imagine anyone stepping on Mary Ellen.

A sharp, angry frown creased Mary Ellen's lovely face. She missed a beat in the music and then whirled, her back to Donny now, dancing with a violence in her movements. Donny immediately turned himself, to see if *he*'d been the cause of that anger or if there was something going on behind him.

There was Nancy Goldstein standing in the doorway.

For one blurred, raging moment, Donny thought Nancy had brought Ben. If she had trespassed like that . . . if she had done the unthinkable and brought Ben Adamson *here*. . . .

But when his eyes focused again, he saw that she was entirely alone. She stood in the shrinking posture of the new kid. Nobody spoke to her. Every cheerleader, whether on purpose or by chance, had his or her back to Nancy.

Only Vanessa said anything to Nancy. Her "Gone all the way so fast?" echoed throughout the room.

Mary Ellen took both of Donny's arms and swung him sideways, so that he could not easily see Nancy. The smile on Mary Ellen's face was very strained.

She mad at Nancy or at me? thought Donny nervously.

He had a sense that it would be all too easy to lose Mary Ellen. There were, after all, a lot of boys eager to go out with her. Patrick Henley, for one. It continued to mystify Donny that Mary Ellen didn't date Patrick. He was glad — but confused — especially since it was impossible not to feel the electricity between those two.

Nancy Goldstein stood at the far end of the huge room and nobody said hello. Nobody waved. Nobody said her name. The room seemed too large. Too big and open even to cross. She felt as if she had never known these people, as if they were the same strangers who had terrified her in Garrison.

They hate me, she thought. I hurt them. I was a symbol of loyalty and I dated the captain of the opposite team. I've lost them.

Now she had done it to herself again. She was

stranded at a *second* party she should never have gone to.

Kerry, who would have welcomed Nancy, never saw her. She was too wrapped up in Pres to think of other human beings. As for Pres, he glanced at Nancy, felt anger, and glanced away, because he did not want anything to spoil the evening. Olivia saw Nancy and thought, Why did I ever like her, anyhow? You can't count on Nancy. Olivia went into the kitchen so as to avoid seeing Nancy.

Felicia Tilford, protecting her upholstery, chandeliers, and Oriental rugs, saw her and was shocked. She still found it embarrassing that her son was a cheerleader, but she had to say one thing for his Varsity Squad — they were a tight-knit group. And now they were not only ignoring Nancy, they were making a *point* of not speaking to her.

Felicia Tilford had snubbed many people in her day and she would continue the practice. But in her own home? An invited guest, standing at her door like a waif even the Salvation Army wouldn't want?

"Pres, dear," his mother said, "I believe Nancy needs something cold to drink. Would you like ginger ale, dear, or Coke?" She went to greet Nancy, pressing her soft cheek lightly against the girl's, and escorted her into the room. Nancy seemed pitifully grateful for the attention.

There were moments when Mrs. Tilford wished

she, too, could be sixteen with the world ahead of her, but this was not one. Whatever agony Nancy was enduring, whatever vendetta the kids had against her, Mrs. Tilford didn't want to know about. As Pres brought the soft drink over to Nancy, his mother slipped out of the room.

Nancy took the glass. It was very cold and it slid in her fingers. She had to put both hands around it. Her hands hurt. I'm holding a glass, she thought, instead of Ben. I'm alone in a room full of my friends.

Pres walked back to Kerry.

Nancy was still alone. She was just closer to the people who were not going to welcome her.

Donny saw, and it stabbed at him.

Memory flooded. Years ago, he was a scrawny, unlovable third grader, going to a birthday party, coming in late, all the other little boys laughing at him. The birthday child saying scornfully, "We only invited you because Mom said we had to, anyhow."

Donny danced Mary Ellen backward toward Nancy. "Hi, Nance," he said. "How are ya?"

It was the best he could do. He kept dancing with Mary Ellen, kept smiling at Nancy.

Nancy burst into tears.

Donny Parrish was horrified. He would gladly have faced Ben Adamson in hand-to-hand combat rather than deal with Nancy Goldstein crying. Donny retreated from those tears faster than he had ever left anything in his life.

But Mary Ellen did not.

Breaking away from Donny's grasp, she went to Nancy. Sisterhood overcame envy and anger. "What happened?" she asked. "Tell me. *Don't cry*. Tarenton cheerleaders don't cry in front of a mob of people." Mary Ellen's voice was stern, but her arms around Nancy were soft and comforting.

Nancy cried harder.

The room divided into those kids who would rather have been dead than get involved, and those kids who would rather have been dead than miss any details.

If it had been Mary Ellen, she would have preferred death to exposure in front of her classmates. She took Nancy's arm more possessively than Ben had ever done, and marched her into the pantry. It was the Victorian part of the house: dark wood, long narrow slivers of cabinets enclosing stacks of rarely used china.

"It was awful," Nancy choked out. "I should never have gone with him. I made him take me home. It was awful."

Mary Ellen hugged her. Nancy thought, If Mary Ellen forgives me, then I guess everyone else will. Everyone who counts, anyhow.

Nancy had loved Ben Adamson. It was a love that lasted only days and consisted of only a few moments of contact, but it was no less real for that. Nancy's throat closed and she could not swallow the soda Mary Ellen wanted her to drink.

Angie was there, handing her a Kleenex, and Olivia was there, looking softer than Olivia Evans could in normal circumstances.

"So it's over? You and Ben?" Mary Ellen said. Nancy nodded.

"Well, let's have a cheer for *that!*" said Mary Ellen, and they all giggled, including Nancy. How like Mary Ellen to go right to the heart of the matter. They'd hated this thing with Ben, and if it was over before it began, then let's all have a cheer.

"*Roadway, runway, railway,*" Angie chanted very softly.

Nancy shook her head. "It didn't even get on the train, let alone go all the way, Angie. I guess we were both at the wrong station at the wrong time." Weeping overcame her again, but this time she was in a knot of friends: girls who cared, girls who wanted her. The tears ended. The lump dissolved.

"Fix your hair," Mary Ellen commanded, handing over a brush. Nancy wanted to laugh. Mary Ellen could not bear it if anyone in the squad looked messy. If you couldn't look good — even in tears — Mary Ellen had no use for you. For Mary Ellen's sake, Nancy brushed her hair. "So," she said, changing the subject, trying to be breezy, "tomorrow night's the big one, huh?"

"We'll whip Garrison," Angie said confidently. "Marc is coming. With him in the crowd I'll be the best cheerleader in the universe. And with me the best cheerleader in the universe, how can we lose?"

They hugged, a circle of love.

In the dark glass of the butler's pantry cabinets, Mary Ellen watched her own reflection. Oh, to have the life of a Tilford — to live where entire rooms were filled with beautiful, useless china and crystal, to have a sink for nothing but arranging the flowers delivered by the greenhouse!

Someday I will, Mary Ellen thought. I'm not a here-today, gone-tomorrow kind of girl. My life will shine. I'm Number One. I'll always be Number One.

She left the girls and walked out to find Donny again, and kissed him fiercely in front of forty spectators. Donny was embarrassed, but Mary Ellen didn't notice. She was rejoicing in her life.

But none of them *really* knew a thing about their future. Whether they would be winners or losers — whether their lives would sparkle in the sun, or darken in the storm.

Even for beautiful cheerleaders, love doesn't last forever. Read Cheerleaders #6, SPLITTING.

If you have enjoyed reading this book in the exciting CHEERLEADERS series look out for the other titles also available now: